Low Key

Robert Shepyer

ISBN: 978-1-62420-441-8

Credits
Cover Artist: Design by Ms G
Editor: Sherry Derr-Wille

Printed in the United States of America

Dedication

To all my friends who love nights filled with wine, cigarettes, and uproarious laughter.

Part I

The Tragic Kingdom

Chapter One

The Imaginary Man

After she read my words, she couldn't love me. If that was how my mind ticked then she must've married the wrong cat. I tried to tell her I was from a different age but she wasn't having it, nothing could excuse my complete lack of literary talent and she would rather be alone than love a hack. Before she left the last time, her parting words to me were, *"Keep it low key"*.

In my Disneyfied mind, Maria mistook me for the perfect Beast to her Belle. The only problem was that Beast was rich and I was poor and Belle loved books while Maria loved film. In actuality, I was more like Quasimodo, which would make sense because Esmeralda never really loved him back.

That's unfair though. There was a time when we loved each other so obsessively I could look at her one certain way and her whole pale body would blush bright pink before melting in my arms. Conversely, Maria was the skeleton key to my mind, body, and soul. Only once she unlocked those trinkets and spent some time inside them, she grew bored with me.

I cannot stress this enough; quantity of pain endured has no relation to quality of love dispensed. That's what our marriage taught us after three years. Maria thought I, Illy Robin, had been through so much pain I was tenderized to the point I could love more deeply than any other. The truth was pain never gave me anything but the ability to endure more pain.

For every decade of my life there's been a different disease or disorder. I was born with Marfan syndrome, a disorder that expresses itself as extremely as the disfiguring wretchedness of the Elephant Man or as subtly cool as the spindly limbed Joey Ramone. Thankfully, I resemble the latter, on the outside.

At five, I was stricken with Idiopathic Thrombocytopenic Purpura. I spent my formative years between babyhood and kidhood in Children's hospital, spotted up and down with brown and purple bruises. All of us damaged goods would sleep in one big quarantine with Disney movies playing through the night on a closed-circuit TV. We neither watched nor slept, we would lie back, stare up at the ceiling and wait for God to answer, "What will become of us?"

By the time I was shipped off to school, I already had an intimate relationship with death. Antisocial and mutated by puberty, I was bullied every day and toughened up to prepare myself for a career in evasion, de-escalation, and sneak. I became a private detective. A dick. Funny thing is, my bully got into investigation too, only he ended up bullying on behalf of the LAPD. There was a time when being a private eye in LA was considered cliché but now, in 2025, it's an anachronism. You'll know it's a police state when there are no more P.I.'s. And yeah, maybe I romanticize my career, getting tattoos of Sam Spade, Phillip Marlowe, and Lew Archer on my stomach and naming my gun Beretta James...

"When she sings, she don't go *bang, bang, bang...* she go *scat, scat, scat.*"

I figure romanticizing gives this lonely beat some purpose.

Maria was the last woman who made love to me and that was three years ago. I've found living without the therapy of sex makes the mind question the reality of every object. I'll jay-walk through a busy street, see a car coming, and stare at the only passenger in the back seat as if daring him to exist. Will this car actually hit me? No, they're not designed to do that, nothing is anymore.

This feeling that envelopes me, this detachment...I cannot pursue the act of love when I am arrested in the condition of love. I feel like an imaginary person...that somehow animated himself.

Chapter Two

Briefly, on Vermin Culture

History consolidates the noteworthy into three categories; heroes, villains, and victims. The hero culture in our movies is in stark contrast to the victim culture of our people. This victim culture was created by the villain class to desensitize and deprive us of the skills we need to serve the modern machine. They are teaching us to fear love because people that don't love don't reproduce.

I imagine the energies collected from all our missed opportunities to seize the moment and kiss the girl have been combining and multiplying into the black hole that will eat the world. All the love that never was is churning, colliding, sucking, and collapsing forever into impotent nothing.

To the villains we were never victims, we were vermin. Ain't it just like the rich to protect the evil that did them good?

Chapter Three

Elastic Chastity

Twenty feet above street level. Sound recording. Camera focused. I'm perched up in a palm tree, squatting, as hidden as a raven in the shadows of the mind. A tree husk is crawling up my ass, but I'm unfazed by this discomfort. I keep it cool in the blazing heat.

I've snapped ten pictures; Dorothy arriving at the scene, lighting a cigarette, smoking it, putting it out on the bottom of her shoe, dealer X arriving, the hand off, the kiss, Dorothy scampering back into the convent, dealer X lighting a cigarette, dealer X's car peeling itself out. "X" isn't code, unless for *douche*, that's actually his name. Dorothy Royce is an American princess hiding from her father, Randolph, to pursue her dreams of sado-activist vagabondage, but before she can jump into that street soup, she has to lay low and who would suspect a dame crazy enough to wear all black in this heat? God have mercy.

I glanced down from my binoculars at myself and remembered I'm no better. Dark blue suit and slacks, white button up, black tie. Chill shades of chill colors absorbing the sun's rays. I've been sweating up here for an hour now, waiting for the moment she walks out to feed the birds.

"Hey man, what the hell are you doing up there?" came a shouting from the street.

It was Carino, an old friend, Hispanic of unspecified origin and a B-famous actor living on the streets. He had long curly hair with eyes as shifty as mercury. He would stay skinny no matter how many six packs he drank. Sometimes a pest, Carino would send me long text messages detailing everything he did and saw on a night out no matter how little I cared.

To Carino, masturbation was an institution, masturbation and drinking. Often, he would jerk off with one hand and hold his beer with the other. He was afraid one day he would confuse the two and accidently end up spilling his beer and taking a sip from his cock.

"You can see me down there?"

Jesus, how long have I been poking out of cover? Is it my knees again, protruding up over my head?

"Illy, you're in a palm tree...I saw you from all the way up the block."

"Stop screaming. I'm undercover."

"Really, who are you snoopin' on?" He lowered his volume but knew some life hack to make his whispers travel long distance s.

"Randolph Royce's daughter, if you must know."

"Ree-he-she-really? How'd you land a gig like that, big shot?"

"Got referred by a friend, now shut up and scram."

The convent doors opened and there she was, a little late, with a bag of seeds in her holy water washed hands and her blank clothes failing to hide that spoiled bourgeoisie edge. The angle of her eyes, the point of her nose and chin, the way her lips clasped like closed scissors, covered a skull whose evil no makeup could conceal. She strolled over to the splatter of shade on the convent's lawn and the birds gathered around. Doves made feral by the times. Carino glanced over to her then back to me.

"That her?"

I nodded like a viper, hissing.

Taking my job into his own crude hands, Carino strutted over to the budding lovely, balancing wealthy confidence and homeless apathy.

"Hell of a day, isn't it?"

"Yes, this blessed heat has been torture for the sisters as well as myself."

"Sisters? Well consider me a convert, because if God made more of you then praise his holy name forever."

"Amen," giggling, she edged closer to him, dropping the bag of seeds for the doves to devour.

"You're cute, do you live around here?"

"Here, there, and everywhere."

She lifted up a finger to curl her hair but realized it was hidden beneath her cap.

"Well, I have a confession to make. I'm not really a nun, I'm just doing this for research."

"Babe, if you want to know the effects long periods of abstinence have on the human body and mind, I know just the cat."

"Does he believe in God?"

"Yeah, all of 'em."

Laughing again, edging closer, her face an inch from his chest to give the impression of touch but the sensation of longing.

"If you want to see what I look like under all these rags, we can meet up tonight."

"That'd be nice, I know a guy who will let us use his shower."

"Take down my number."

Carino pulled out his phone to jot down her digits.

"310-458-8515, I'm Dorothy."

"I'm Carino, let's meet up at the loneliest hour."

"One it is."

Smirking, she took that unforgiving step back, like pulling out a meat-hook lodged in him, and with one teasing swoop, she spun on her heel and sashayed back into the convent. Carino reached down, grabbed the bag of seeds to eat and walked back to me. I shimmied down the tree to meet him on equal ground.

"You should hire me full time...did you see that?"

"Don't give yourself too much credit, she's easy."

"Oh, like you could do better?"

"We're gonna find out."

"What do you mean?"

"You're going to set up a time to meet her but I'm going to be there instead of you to talk her into coming back home to her father."

"What makes you think I'd ever pass on pussy I earned?"

"Think of all the times you got drunk on my dime when you were broke. All the people I talked out of kicking your ass...I'm asking for a favor but call it a demand."

"Geez, why is it always checks and balances with you? Fine, have her. If this works, then I get half of what Randolph's paying you."

"No way, that's rent."

"Fine, then I get to crash on your couch."

"I sold it."

"Fine, not only does my tab with you get wiped clean but now you're in *my* debt, so when the time comes I ask you for a favor, you have to accept it."

I paused the moment and let it sink in, to be cemented in time. Barely breaking the silent stillness, the breathless silence, I put my hand out and Carino shook it. The city sensed the score was settled and cooled down as if the Gods turned the temperature and contrast dials to give the blue-black night a tranquil under glow. They spoke inside a breeze, *"It's all good."*

"Deal," I agreed.

~ * ~

Carino instructed Dorothy to meet at Chip's diner in Highland Park at one a.m. Choosing to meet at a restaurant aroused her suspicion but she just went with it, high off anticipation.

Are you sure you're poor? she texted Carino.

Chip's wasn't the Ritz but they reserved the right to refuse any customer. No restaurant would accept Carino stinking up their booths, scaring the squares. That's just the way things are now, the poor can't find a place to sit down and eat in peace.

One a.m. rolled around like a pair of sarcastic eyes, and I saw Dorothy sitting in a plush green booth wearing a posh red dress. I stood outside, smoking a Camel down to the butt to give myself the time to really observe every nuance that made up Dorothy. You can learn a lot about someone just by watching them wait. Dorothy was a nail biter, a hair chewer, a bang her head on the table in plain public kind of gal, a child. I stepped into Chip's and slithered over to her table.

"Dorothy?"

"You were the creep trying to hide in the palm tree, what do you want?"

"Just to talk."

"Not to me, Gonzo...I'm meeting someone, so unless you want them to kick your ass, I suggest you get up."

A waiter that must've sailored every morning and lumber-jacked on weekends, moseyed over, crossing his thick anchor tattooed arms over his flannel covered chest.

"Excuse me miss, is this man bothering you?"

"Yes, get him out of my booth please."

He grabbed my arm and swiftly lifted me out of my seat.

"Alright, butterscotch, let's go," he instructed me.

"I've been hired by your father to bring you home, Dorothy," I then turned to the waiter, "That's Randolph Royce, you want me to lose his daughter and get this place turned into a strip mall?"

The waiter hesitated, his beard quivered as he turned to Dorothy for help.

"Put him down. I'll deal with this," she gave in.

I pulled my arm out of the waiter's grasp and sat back down.

"Sorry, sir, I had no idea you were here on business."

"I'll take three slices of garlic bread and a chopped liver special, hold the lettuce and if it's not on the house, then you'll lose the house."

"And two strawberry milk shakes," Dorothy added.

"Make it four," I multiplied.

"Coming right up," he bowed and ran to the kitchen.

She recalibrated her eyes on me. I wasn't the type she expected.

"What's my father doing hiring a schlub like you?"

"Mr. Royce knows I'm the best in my line of work. It was either me or the cops. He would've rather lost you than hired them."

"What's your name?"

I pulled my blue card out of my blue suit pocket and slid it across the table.

"Illy Robin, private eye... Illy?" she asked, giving me a puzzled look.

"Real name's Ilya, it's Russian."

"Look Illy, I'm an adult woman, I can make my own decisions and the last place I'd ever choose to be is back in my father's house."

"Why's that?"

"The smell. The reek of greed is death. Down with the people it smells like life and life's all I got time for."

"Look miss, not everyone is as lucky as you to be born into fortune. If you want to reject it, go ahead but don't go sticking your nose in dangerous circles of people that only want to exploit you. The grass ain't always greener. Be grateful and use your resources."

"Gratitude would be masochistic...but you're right. I'm in trouble, Illy."

"What kind of trouble?"

"X found out about Carino and he was going to come here and kick his ass. Now that you're here instead, he's probably just going to make fun of you since he'd never lay a hand on anyone working for my dad."

"Sticks and stones," I shrugged.

Her eyes floated up over my head as X entered the diner, twirling a crowbar in his hand. I followed her line of sight and turned around to see X standing over me.

"Bitch, I thought you said he was a poor Mexican."

"Nope, middle class Russian, hired by her father," I corrected him.

X sighed and put the crowbar down on the table.

"Is Mr. Royce here?" X cowardly questioned.

Paying his weakness no mind to deflate it further, I turned to Dorothy.

"Is he your boyfriend, Dorothy?"

Scared out of her wits, she tried shaking her head but the fear screwed her neck in too tightly.

"See, you don't own her, you're just obsessed and pathetic," I told X.

"Yeah well, you're an ugly, weird looking commie Jew, and I bet you couldn't get laid if you tried."

"Yeah...pretty much," I nodded and smiled, staring at X until he looked away and down and shrunk to the size of a prize I could win from the diner's mechanical arm machine.

"Look girl, I'll be waiting outside," X told Dorothy, defeated and fooling himself.

"Don't waste your time, I'm taking her back home and if you ever contact her again, I will give the cops all the pictures I have of you selling dope to kids."

"I guess this is goodbye, Dorothy," X grabbed his crowbar and sulked out of the diner.

The restaurant returned to peaceful chitter-chatter, but I felt like I deserved an applause.

"How did you do that?" Dorothy was amazed.

"When you look like I do, people don't want to bother you... It's amazing what you can get away with."

The waiter returned with our food, meticulously setting every drink and dish in front of us in the most aesthetically pleasing placement.

"Can we take this to go?" I asked.

Fury bubbled beneath the gloss of politeness on the waiter's face. I could see his scalp angrily suck up the gel in his hair. "Sure, let me wrap this up for you, and again, I'm so sorry about how I behaved earlier. We would love to have you here anytime, next meals on the house too."

"Thanks, bitch."

He smiled through clenched teeth then took our food back to wrap up.

"Are you going home or not?"

Dorothy sighed with every bit of tension her failed activist dreams accumulated, "Fine."

Stepping out of Chip's with four strawberry milkshakes and a bag of food, we strolled into the parking lot where we caught X just outside of a street light's reach, getting beaten bloody by a man shrouded in darkness.

X was tough enough not to fall but slow enough to be battered with strike after strike. A jab to the jaw, a knee to the stomach, an elbow to the temple, he was spraying the street with blood then sprinkling it with teeth. Whoever this man shrouded in darkness was, he fought like a poor boy, a real slugger.

"Good riddance," I shrugged.

Dorothy and I walked over to my blue Cadillac and she instinctively pulled at the back-door's handle.

"It's not self-driving, take the front."

"*Who are you?*" she asked, befuddled.

We got in. I turned my key in the ignition, put my hand on the gear shift and heard a helicopter chopping from above. I turned to see its searchlight panning the street, and I put my car in reverse to leave before the drama cramped my style. My wheels only rolled back an inch before a swarm of siren screaming cop cars bombarded the lot with one parking right behind me and blocking me in.

"Damn it, no way am I getting trapped in here," I shouted.

X finally dropped to the ground as the man in the darkness realized he could only throw one final punch before having to split. He sprinted to the wall and hopped it in an instant, escaping the cops to fight another day.

"Peace," he barked from behind the wall.

Before he jumped, I caught a brief ID on his long curly locks through my back window. It was Carino.

The backdoor of the armored black and white blocking me opened and out stepped my old friend, Detective Vic Spinoza. He groaned, visibly perturbed then gave his men their orders.

"Two units, cruise into the alley, he won't get far. Jonny and Fitzsimmons will hop the wall and run after him."

Before returning to his car, Spinoza looked my way, seeing right through my back-window's tint then scratched an itch on his nose with his middle finger.

"Peckerwood...let's get out of here," I said to Dorothy.

"How?" Dorothy asked.

I put the car in drive, turned the wheel as severely as I could and stepped on the gas. In a split, we turned ninety degrees and I drove over Chip's lawn and through a bush to get out of the lot.

"Driving isn't for robots and it certainly isn't for tools."

"You're crazy, won't they follow you?"

"Spinoza knows better than that."

We crept up the streets, people-watching the homeless and their rain dances until we met the Pasadena hills where the only life stirring were the animals. I climbed the roads all the way to the top where Randolph Royce rested his head.

~ * ~

His doorbell sounded more like a gong. It was now four thirty a.m. Thirty minutes after his alarm. He answered the door already in a suit, sipping from a coffee mug that read *World's Richest Dad* and turned to Dorothy without acknowledging me. Randolph Royce had a piggy bank pink body that stored fat like coins. His ginger locks and bushy moustache and eye brows made it known that he came from old wealth, three generations removed. Every gesture looked expensive and invited envy.

"This has to be the last time, Dorothy. A wealthy Chinaman I know saw you on the street looking like a complete floozy, and now he's hesitating to answer my calls. Is that how you return the favor for raising you with a golden spoon in your mouth?"

"Sorry, Dad."

"Go to your room, it's just how you left it but take your shoes off, they look filthy."

Dorothy slipped her shoes off and stepped inside, cruising right to her quarters. Randolph then took a good look at me with his tongue pressing against the inside of his cheek, trying to get a gauge on how to repay me.

"Come inside, Illy. Let Suzanne make you coffee."

I walked in and he shut the door.

The Espresso King shat out my joe into a mug that Randolph's maid Suzanne brought to me in his office where I sat under his security guard's shadow. Dante was so muscle-bound you could see his veins protruding through his clothes, trickling down from his head to his feet. A German Luger rested on his waist and he never took his finger off the trigger. I took a sip of the espresso and felt a single hair sprout on my balls. Randolph sat in a gold leather chair, swiveling back and forth. "You're not the luckiest guy in the world, are ya?"

"No sir, I've had many curses on my head."

"Yet, that never stopped you from delivering the goods, did it?"

"Never, sir."

"There ought to be some justice for that, don't you think? If God won't do it, I will."

"There's been justice, only the kind that rewards me by smiting others."

"I'm going to reward you by empowering you, Illy."

"We agreed upon ten thousand dollars, not some self-help hoodoo."

"Ten thousand? That's all? Sheesh, Uncle Same, as I like to call the commie-welfare-state-bastard, squeezes much more out of me in taxes, but the LAPD wouldn't lift a finger to find my daughter unless it was up her skirt. That's why I hired you and Dante over here. I investigate and secure myself privately."

"Don't even get me started on the LAPD. There's this one detective, Vic Spinoza, you ever heard of him?"

"No, and please don't bring him up again..." he paused for a moment, rocking in his chair. "You like women, right? You're no goo-gobbler."

"Yeah, women."

"Good, I am going to set you up on some dates."

"Really?"

"Yes, with good girls too. Girls I've known carnally and would recommend any day. They will take care of you as long as they know you're connected to me."

"Are they hookers?"

"No, I'd never pay for sex, not for me or anybody. Now that doesn't mean they don't expect some kind of monetary reward for their troubles, but if they know you're with me, they'll think you're rich."

"I'm not rich."

"No shit, Shylock Holmes, but they don't need to know that."

"How will I afford to take them out?"

"I'll pay for everything; food, drinks, drugs, whatever you need...and I'll get someone to plan out each date, a professional."

"Where's the authenticity in that?"

"Illy...it's 2025...stop thinking like a sap."

"Try to find women that appreciate sappy."

"There are none."

"Alright, I give in. Sign me up."

"Your first date will be on Friday night. Don't dress like a goof."

"I'll try."

"I will even the scales, Illy. All the hardship you've had to endure is coming to an end. I am the light at the end of your tunnel. You're finally going to get what you deserve."

"Love?"

Randolph Royce laughed so hard that his gut almost breached through his shirt.

"No, *self-love*. I'm not doing this for the girls, I'm doing this for you. It all comes down to how they make *you* feel," Randolph leaned back into his chair, pleased to spread the disease.

"Amen," Dante added.

I drove home and got to bed around six a.m. The sun was coming up to torture the poor. I needed to sleep through the day and pretend everything would be alright in the world. At least there was hope for me.

Chapter Four

Maria: Esmeralda

The sunset was warming my window, begging me to pay it mind from behind my venetian blinds.

Geez, Illy, sometimes you get too carried away, I thought to myself, sweating in bed. I mean hell, I've probably imagined proposing to every woman I've ever met. Sometimes, I do it in a hot air balloon. Other times, at the top of the Eifel tower. With Dorothy, I imagined asking her to marry me while lying on top of her on Randolph's desk. Not that I have any interest in Dorothy.

Is self-love really what I deserve? Not *love* love...but isn't one dependent on the other? If you ask my ex, she would say I have boat-loads of self-love...because that's just a euphemism for ego, right? She saw the narcissism within my self-loathing. I hate myself because I'm all I think about. Or maybe not, maybe she taught me to hate myself. See how love fucks you up? I must hate my....

I don't even want to say it...

...Self. I went back to sleep.

~ * ~

Blue slacks today. Blue suit. White button up. Black tie. Off to the office I go. I drive through Highland Park beside rich road cholos in low riders, their hydraulics making the broke sidewalk cholos jealous. They see me driving and think I must be some kind of oddball.

My office is dimly lit with wooden floors and blue walls and source-less smoke in the air. I think it rises up from the crematorium downstairs. I put down my bag and sit in my swivel chair. I plop my legs down on my desk, hands behind my head, getting to work which means staying in this position, day dream about my cases and my writing, killing two birds with one stone. Without a case on hand, prose came to mind.

Men fantasize and women narrativize.

Woe unto youth.

Young men not seeing a woman's soul through her eyes and young women not seeing men in the first act of their lives.

I might use that in my novel. It's going to about a guy on death row who—

That was when a tapping came a-rapping on my door's frosted window.

"Come in."

She opened the door and walked back into my life. She was wearing a black and red polka-dot blouse and had grown out her bangs, which meant she was in mourning. She always liked to dress vintage-LA-darkside. In fact, part of the reason she ever dated me was because I looked like I was haunted.

"Maria..."

"This is one of the hardest things I've ever had to do, but I didn't know who else to turn to."

"Are you in trouble?"

"I think I'm safe but you never know... It's my husband... You remember David."

"Maria York... Does that really sound better than Maria Robin? What makes you think I'd stick my neck out for his ass? My own divorce lawyer, fucking my wife during the proceedings then MARRYING HER.... He negotiated a good deal for you, huh? Really made that fine print small. If he needs a private eye, why couldn't he ask me himself? Shows what kind of man you chose."

"Because he's dead, Illy," she peeped, holding her tears back so hard she almost drowned. Deep down I thought she was acting.

"Really? How?"

"He was murdered. They found him on the corner of 6th and San Pedro in the gutter like a dog."

"I'm so sorry."

"No, you're not...but I don't care, I just want your help."

"To find out who killed him?"

She let the tears flow, unembarrassed. She then threw down a thick manila folder on my desk. Page one was an eight by eleven glossy photograph of York, dead as rusty nails. His throat had been sliced open cleanly and part of his esophagus was flapping out of his neck to prop a Cuban cigar, a Pacifica, inside the organ.

"He was unapologetically capitalist. The Cuban cigar was their sick version of an insult."

"He liked to play the stocks, huh?"

"We rang the Nasdaq bell at his funeral."

"I wouldn't assume he was murdered over a difference in economic philosophy."

"Can you think of a motive?"

"Didn't he used to eat with his mouth open? Maybe someone got offended?" I joked, but she didn't find it funny.

"You're my only hope, Illy."

I flipped past the photograph and looked at all the print she had beneath it. Everything from dentists' notes to music sheets of songs he wrote for her, the guy's whole life. One of the songs was called "My Darling Dear."

My Darling Dear
In your eyes, I see clear
The meaning of me, the meaning of life
Me as your husband, you as my wife
Sharing love together, sharing love as one
On my dying day, I'll be gone but I'd have won

"I thought you said you'd never love a hack."

"It's better than anything you ever wrote," she spat back and I laughed.

"Only kidding...my bottom rate is five thousand to start."

"After paying the funeral expenses and with my unemployment..."

"Say no more, I'll put you on a payment plan."

"I was hoping you could do this for me as a favor."

"That wouldn't be very capitalist of me, now would it?"

I leaned back in my chair maybe to think or maybe for her to notice my crotch, probably both. That expression always gets me, when she tries on different attitudes but ends up going completely blank.

"Were you cheating on him?"

She silently stared holes into my head, but I deflected her gaze with one well curled eye brow.

"He couldn't get it up...and you know how I get," she said.

I nodded, sympathetically.

"I need you to tell me everything about the last day of David York's life.

"We had an argument in the morning because I wanted him to take the day off for a beach outing. When he refused, I asked him to leave me some money so I could go shopping. He left me only a thousand dollars and I demeaned him so terribly, he actually cried. He didn't come home that night after work, so I called his secretary, Joan, and she told me he went to Johnny's bar."

"At least he had good taste in dives."

"According to the bartender, he stayed at Johnny's for three drinks. It was only David, the bartender and the owner in the building and that's the last anyone saw or heard of him."

I set my feet flat on the floor and leaned forward, pursing my lip and caressing my chin to think. This was too good to be true. My ex coming back to me and my nemesis dead. There had to be a catch.

"Is LAPD on the case?"

"Where do you think I got the picture? They can't do what you do though."

"Which detective?"

"Spinoza."

"You're damn right he can't do me. I was going to sleep on it but now I have to take this case."

"Because your bully is on it too?"

"Yes."

"This is about being a man now? Not about my late husband?"

"It's always about being a man, even if that makes me a fool."

"Whatever, the ends justify the means."

Before she left my office, she had one last bit of shaming for me.

"I'll never forgive you for making me a realist," she lamented then slowly sulked out.

I thought about taking the case slow, drawing it out, pulling Maria closer to me with every call and drink we shared to discuss it. I could tell she had the opposite of a crush on me, like what a crush is to love, this was to hate. Meanwhile, my menstruating heart still bled for her. I love her, don't I? So much that I'd rather hate her than love someone else.

I was so shaken by our reunion, I had to step outside for a smoke.

Chapter Five

Damnation of the Beggars

The homeless took the sidewalks and the rich took the roads. It was only a decade ago that every class shared the streets, but with the innovation of the self-driving automobile, the greatest shift of structural unemployment in American history occurred and millions were kicked to the curb and forced into homelessness. So many people were living on the street that confrontation with them was unavoidable. You can't just walk past a beggar and pretend they don't exist anymore. So rather than offering a helping hand, the rich collectively decided to stop using the sidewalks and claim the road.

With their great numbers, the homeless decided to rally and fight their oppressor, but all they accomplished was rousing themselves up to the point that eateries, shops, and markets refused to serve them. The government started subsidizing meals for the homeless with self-service food trucks that would park by homeless encampments three times a day to feed everyone. The food tasted like cardboard, but it filled you up and at least it didn't look toxic, though by all logic it was.

The worst thing about being homeless in Los Angeles isn't the starvation or humiliation, it's the weather. No rain and unforgiving sun all year round.

I needed to sweat Maria out and smoke a cigarette. There was a food truck parked right on the corner and a line up the block of men, women, children, and Carino waiting to be fed. People in the line recognized Carino from television and gathered around him for autographs. He signed them, not asking for a dime even though he could've. Carino was living proof that Hollywood million-dollar pay checks were a fantasy. I walked down the line toward Carino but was stopped by a homeless man that had half his face burned off. His hands were cupped in front of his chin, begging.

"Please, *please*, PLEASE."

He was worth getting a good look at. The left side of his face was so disfigured by fire that I felt a sizzle on my tongue.

"I will give you twenty dollars if you tell me what happened to you."

The homeless man started crying. Saplings and tears ran down his face and into his cupped hands as if they were his charity.

"I...I...I was a mule, supposed to hand off a couple kilos but I forgot where I hid da bricks and lost 'em...then when I came back to boss man, he...he...he..."

"What the hell is wrong with you? Did your mother drop you and fracture your skull when you were a baby, you fucking retard?"

Crying harder now, "He stuck my head on the stove so hard that my face fried up like an egg."

"There, there, here's twenty," I said while leaving a bill in his hands.

He wiped his tears away and I tried to leave his side but he grabbed me by the sleeve and stopped me.

"My name is Monty Freed, so in case I die today at least you would have known my name."

"Thanks."

I pulled away from him and continued down the line seeing representatives from every color and creed, because class assumed the social function of race to divide Angelinos. The rich blacks, whites, and Latinos united to hate the poor blacks, whites, and Latinos.

Wheeling a little red wagon filled to the brim with liquor bottles was the Highland Park Booze Hound. Each neighborhood had one, a designated fetcher of spirits that could get a poor man any drink he wanted without having to beg for entry to a market.

"Sale on rum. Sale on vodka. Liquidation on liquid dinner. Got a strange six pack of beers imported right from the golden goose's ass in Thailand," the booze hound heralded.

I kept walking until finally I reached Carino. He was among his fans.

"Hey, I saw you last night at Chip's, kicking X's ass," I informed Carino.

"You beat someone up, Carino? Wow, that's so cool," one of his younger fans glowed.

"It sure is, my boy...he started it though." Carino raised his eyes up from the boy back to me. "You know how I am, Illy. So leisurely it drives people to fits of jealous rage...but what are you doing here with us, anyway? You just got paid ten thousand dollars, shouldn't you be in a helicopter or something?"

"So, just because I earn some dough means I can't be around my poor friends anymore?"

"Yes...you work for Royce, the worst villain of them all. You have to pick a side, dude."

"We need an ambassador to take them down, don't we?" I reasoned.

"No one likes a friend to all...I say we just burn the whole town to the ground, HOW 'BOUT THAT EVERYBODY?"

Everyone cheered and raised a fist in solidarity with Carino. He found himself at the front of the line and ordered a tuna melt on the menu screen and one was dispensed in seconds.

"Why don't you eat that in my office? I've got AC."

"No thanks, deep pockets. I know how your kind operates, I accept the offer and the one favor you owe me goes *poof!* gone."

"I just want to go somewhere a little more tranquil."

"There's an alley I know, lots of shade, real quiet."

"Lead the way."

Carino took me to his secret alley, where the walls were spray painted with the slogan of our time, *EAT THE RICH*. Often imitated, this was an original piece with the proper signature, Rawr. Whoever Rawr was, he was a hero to the people and the only source for news on the street.

Chapter Six

Beverly: Anastasia

Early Friday. A blink before dawn. In the black matter of my sleeping brain I can feel the electrical current of a thought fizzing into existence. *Start Maria's case today but make sure to leave enough time to pull yourself together for your first blind date.* I heard a buzzing and woke up to a text message from Randolph Royce.

Wake up, your ride will be arriving in five minutes.

What could he possibly want this early? I got out of bed, took a two-minute shower and dressed for the remaining three minutes until I heard a honking come from an empty Escalade in my apartment's driveway. I slackered out of my complex and got in the SUV for a smooth and mathematical ride to Randolph Royce's personal barbershop. When the car arrived, a man-servant was there to open my door and greet me. Randolph's barber was an old timey type with a white moustache and plenty of wax to curl your intrigue.

"Mr. Royce has instructed me to give you the crescendo cut."

"What's that?"

The barber pointed to a picture of a perfectly combed, white-bread trim with a single curl crescendoing down the forehead. Parted down the side, each wave elegantly crested over a face like fresh rain. After ten minutes, it looked like the barber had shaved down my skull into a more pleasing shape.

I swooped out of the barbershop and the Escalade's next stop for me was Randolph Royce's tailor. An ancient Italiano named Luciano had owned and operated this little hole in the wall for forty years. With artisan craftsmanship, he tailored a gray suit for me, threading his needle into every loose fold and stiff stretch. I felt that feeling that must eat good people up when they get wealthy, like I had something to rub in people's faces now. Once finished, a man-servant carried my new suit into the car and I was taken to Royce's spa. A collective of concubines gave me the full treatment: facials, skin softening, full body massage with oil in nothing but a towel.

"You want happy ending or sad beginning?" said one masseuse.

"What's the sad beginning?"

"You eat me out."

"What's so sad about that?"

"That's just what Mr. Royce calls it."

I went straight home to get ready for my date. I was so nervous, I spoiled I'd undone all of Royce's efforts to make me presentable. My muscles were tensing, my hair was frizzing out, and my suit was loosening up and unthreading. I received a text.

The escalade will take you to Beverly Hills to pick her up then to a private event where there will be some very important people. Act cool and casual but don't slouch or curse and make sure to speak up…plus wear a rubber.

What kind of private event is it?

Solstice party.

The Escalade drove me up the winding wealth warp of Beverly Hills. There was mansion after mansion after mansion until finally just a house where she was waiting. She was a moon kissed brunette with light olive skin and a face that gave away her Eastern European heritage.

I stepped out the car to meet her.

"Hi, I'm Illy."

"I'm Beverly, nice to meet you."

"Likewise, shall we?"

Beverly hopped in the Escalade with me and on we went crawling up the hill to the summit.

"What's your story? How do you know Randolph?" she asked me.

"We're business associates."

"That's it? That's your story?"

"I'm a thirty-four-year-old divorced private investigator with Marfan syndrome."

"Boooooring."

"I agree...what about you? Who's Beverly?"

"I'm not sure, I stole the name from the neighborhood."

"You chose your own name?"

"Yeah, I had amnesia so instead of trying to be who I was, I rebranded the whole package."

"Interesting, how'd you get amnesia?"

"Overdose."

"Before that what was your name?"

"Are you stupid or something? I said I had amnesia, I don't remember."

"Right, you *HAD* it."

"What was that syndrome you had again?"

"Marfan...sorry... Do you like living in the Hills, Beverly?"

"Oh, my god. Hate it. So lame."

"Why?"

"People around here don't know how to have a good time, too self-conscious. Just because you can afford good drugs doesn't mean you know what to properly do with your high."

"So why stay?"

"My parents. I live with them."

I couldn't help but connect the dots and label her an Anastasia. Though not a top tier Disney flick, she was a princess nonetheless. Anastasia forgot her royal youth and lived like a tramp till she threw another chance at those riches away to marry another tramp. Anastasias are bossy little nihilists who can assimilate into the public without anyone realizing they're in the presence of royalty. They're also deviously sexy.

We reached a gate covered in ivy and summer colored fungi that crept open for us to drive up to a French style villa as the rust colored sun set behind the rustic architecture. The Escalade passed the front of the villa to the back where it stopped at what seemed to be a forest. I exited the SUV, opened the door, and held my hand out for the princess. She insisted on exiting herself on the other side. We trotted down the forest trail with both of our expensive black shoes getting dirtied and dusted up. The trail led to a perfectly flat landscape with a hedge maze. Standing by the maze's entrance were two guards dressed in ornate yellow robes, holding Bunsen flame blue torches.

"Welcome to the solstice, you'll be needing this."

Beverly opened up her palm and the guard handed her a compass.

"This will guide your way," the guard assured us.

Beverly was thrilled, staring down at the device in her hands, tinkering with it.

"Wait...a compass...in a maze? How would that help?"

"It tells us what direction we're going, stupid," Beverly said.

"Yeah, but we don't need to know our direction, we need to know our way."

"Jesus, what syndrome did you say you were born with again?"

"Marfan."

"Okay Marvin, so let me do the navigating." The compass, which was broken, read south. "It's this way, follow me."

Beverly ran ahead and took the first turn southward. The next fork was between west and east and she winged it toward the west. *West coast is the best coast*, she must have figured. Leading to a wall of green, two yellow robed guards poked up from behind the hedges and poured buckets of ice water over our heads as punishment for reaching the dead-end.

"Try again, summer saps!" they cackled and hid back behind the hedge.

Soaking wet, a squish with every step, we headed back east until the next fork in the maze, this time having to choose between north and south again.

"The compass says south."

I grabbed the compass out of her hand and flung it as hard as I could over the wall.

"What the hell. How are we going to find our way now?"

"We'll just have to guess now, won't we?"

I saw Beverly squint. She noticed something small and far off down the north path.

"Maybe not."

Beverly dashed over to something in the grass and picked it up. I came closer and saw she was holding a pill in her hand. There was a trail of them, coming in every color, leading down the maze.

"Someone was nice enough to make a trail."

"I hope you're not thinking of taking that."

She popped it into her mouth with total indifference.

"Beverly, you don't even know what that was?"

"I can imagine...but still I'm hoping for a surprise."

"After overdosing and losing your memory, you still..."

"There's nothing still about me, Illy. I'm completely new."

Beverly ran off, picking up and popping every pill along the maze. I ran after her until we both arrived at the entrance to the solstice party where we were welcomed by a morning jazz quartet and a chorus of mingling by guests dressed in soaking wet fine clothes. There was a buffet of food and open bar. There was a garden of earthly delights decorated with orchids, lilies, tulips, and birds of paradise in both the flower and animal variety.

"See, you should've listened to me all along," Beverly proudly puffed.

"You're right, I'm sorry."

"You can make it up to me by getting me a vodka double, straight."

"Will do."

I lit a cigarette and sashayed over to the open bar, letting my gallop match the jazz's rhythm. The bartender, dressed in a white shirt with yellow bowtie and suspenders, whipped up a Stoli vodka double and a Jameson on the rocks for me. I grabbed our two drinks, keeping my cig hanging off my lip, when I was stopped by a hard-boiled stiff in a crispy black suit with a brick shaped head under a fedora and black rimmed glasses.

"Sir, you can't smoke here," he told me.

"Oh, please forgive me...are you the owner of the estate?"

"No, just a goddamn good Samaritan." We stared each other in a match of mental judo. "Are you going to put it out or am I going to have to turn that cigarette into chewing tobacco for you?"

I could see him playing out violent scenarios of my death in his head.

"Fine."

I was about to throw my cigarette away, but he took it out of my mouth for me and dropped it in my whiskey.

"You gonna get me another drink?" I asked as I tossed the liquid.

"Sorry, dear, I already have a date."

"I'm no man's dear. I'm Detective Illy Robin."

"You may call me the Ticking Man," he said with his hand over his chest and a smile on his face as if he was overjoyed to make the acquaintanceship of a new and formidable rival.

Though we were far from finished, he walked past me, almost through me, to a myriad of beautiful women that smiled and laughed as they welcomed him.

"Asshole..." I sneered to myself.

I looked back over to where I left Beverly and discovered she was missing. My heart sank.

"Oh no."

I scanned the grounds, looking for her. Left, right, over, under, she was nowhere to be found...but then I saw a rather royal looking ass protruding out from behind a table so I ran and found Beverly hunched over, puking into a metal bucket.

"Beverly, are you alright?"

"No...water...please..." her voice sounded burnt by her stomach's acids.

I searched for a water bottle...or an ice cube...anything. While I wasn't looking, Beverly snatched the vodka double out of my hand. She threw her head back and sent the liquid down her throat.

"Beverly, that wasn't water, that was..."

"*Ahhh*...thank you, that's so much better," she interrupted, refreshed.

Like nothing, she wiped the vomit wash off of her lips and onto her sleeve then followed the music that only she could hear. I needed to stay by her side but...

"You," I heard a raspy voice and turned in its direction.

The voice belonged to a beautiful woman. Though only thirty, her premature wrinkles seemed to hide secret wisdom. When she came closer, I noticed paint all over her clothes and body, both wet and dry. She gave off the feel that her spirit was too powerful to be confined to a material prison, whether that be her body or the entire world.

"I have to paint your portrait. I got all the materials right here. They hired me to do that for guests and usually they come to me, but a face like yours appears once in a lifetime. You're beautiful."

"I don't see the harm...why not?"

"Thank you."

She jumped in for a hug, forgetting the wet paint on her clothes so when she pulled away, my new suit went from Hugo Boss to Jackson Pollock. The hug momentarily transported us to the top of Mount Everest where we were freezing to death and our only warmth was in each other's arms. In the last moment of our lives, we both said, "I love you," then froze into the same block of ice. Back to reality, she had already started walking toward the canvas. I hurried up to her side.

"Sorry, I'm Illy, what's your name?"

"Rocky...Rocky Rude."

"You really think I'm handsome?"

"Not handsome, but beautiful...I could cry the most tender tears of joy out of my right eye and sadness out of my left just looking at you...you remind me of all the damage I overcame trying to get paid to paint."

"How long have you been painting?"

"Twenty-five years, the first ten I only did graffiti."

We arrived at her canvas where there was a stool for me to perch my ass. I sat down and she took her brush and palette and sized me up, tongue and thumb sticking out. Like a classical composer, she painted music with every color; dabbing, splattering, and stroking sound and sense into image. I sat like a statue hoping she was developing a Pygmalion complex.

"If I was the last woman on Earth and you found me, took me somewhere where there was a lever that if you pulled it, it could kill every other man in the world, would you pull it?"

"Killing billions of people...? I dunno, would you if the situation were reversed and billions of women were killed so they couldn't get to me?"

"You don't have to reverse it, I would do it either way...and I bet if we were really in that situation, you would fight me to pull it.

I had to steer the conversation away from her crazy ravings.

"How's the portrait coming?"

"See for yourself."

She turned the canvas around and I saw a perfect photographic reproduction of myself and for the first time, I truly believed I was attractive.

"Are you single, Rocky?"

"On the rebound and lookin' to score...you?"

"Divorced and solo."

"Take my number down, if I don't see you again, Illy...I'll kill myself...310-510-0225," her threat weighed down what would otherwise be a light sentence.

I dialed in her number and held my phone tight and close. I didn't care if she was a psychopath, I was desperate and knew I could roll with any punches she could throw; stalking, threats, finding a boiling cat on my stove, anything.

I stood up off my stool, slowly walked over to her and leaned in close. Her smile revealed her brown and broken teeth which were hot in a punk rock kind of way, as if to love her would christen me as the king of trash.

"Slow down...for now, you're nothing but a muse to me," she said.

"When can I see you again?"

"I have an art show next week for a new collection of portraits. Plenty of wealthy patrons will be there."

"But only one muse." I smoothly stepped away with one long pimp leg. In the distance, I saw Beverly locking lips with none other than the Ticking Man. I hung over her shoulder to light a cigarette and blew a cloud of smoke in their faces. Beverly pulled away from his lips and smiled at me.

"Gimme one."

"May I give the lady a cigarette?"

"Hmph," he just smiled, then said, "B44."

"What is that supposed to mean? Be forty-four? I'm thirty-four."

The Ticking Man stepped back as if being pulled into the hedge wall and sunk through it, accepted by the bush, twigs making way for him. He was absorbed, hopefully to the other side.

"Where'd he go?" Beverly asked.

"Who cares?"

"Oh, I forgot to tell you. You won't believe this but I remember everything. I'm cured. My name's actually Millie and I'm a model."

"You ready to go?" I asked, unimpressed and over the bull shit.

We made our way through the maze the same way we came then took the Escalade back to her house. I checked my watch after dropping her off, she got home before midnight.

~ * ~

Homicide Report for Millie Glupnick by Detective Vic Spinoza 6-21-25

Body discovered by father of the deceased at eleven forty-eight p.m. Father is famous poet Penn Glupnick. His account of the scene goes as follows:

She rang the doorbell while I was in bed watching PBS. I usually never stay up this late but Geraldo was interviewing Connor McGregor and I had enjoyed his memoir. I got out of bed without waking my wife and answered the door to see Millie standing there, foggy eyed and without expression. I asked her where she was, who she had been with, what was wrong. My daughter was a typical LA night hawk, you see. Strange girl, loved to mess with people, only people ended up messing with her. At first, I thought she was playing a prank then I saw my baby's blood running down her leg. I took two steps around her, after the first I could see the gushing, after the second I saw the tip of her vertebrae sticking out of a hole in the back of her neck. I snapped awake and grabbed her but she was already dead. Her eyes rolled into the back of her benign brain and she fell into my arms, totally limp. I'm still not sure if she was dead that entire time or if she'd seen me.

Father is potential suspect. Weapon used to slice her was steel based blade. Finger prints from doorbell still at the lab. Footprints found at the scene coming from the street. Italian boot by Gizmo size twelve and a half. Footprint has interesting insignia, winking man's face with a landing strip moustache from nose to lip. Is that you, Adolf? Potential links to David York case. Different weapon, foot print, victim sex, but same feeling...same artist.

~ * ~

It's twelve thirty-four p.m. and I'm awake in bed when Carino sends me a text message.

I collected $32.60 today. It was a good day. I used the money to buy a six pack of Kronnenberg from the Booze Hound. He charges 2 dollars more than the liquor store and that ain't right...but I guess even the Booze Hound has to make a living, right Papa? I climbed up a trail to watch a show at the Greek Theatre from the hills, the Roman Bigsby Jazz Experience, you ever heard of 'em? Pretty smooth. There were some other people taking advantage of the free view...I thought I was the only one that knew about this spot. Guess, they must've followed me...fuckers. I drank the six-pack slow and kept having to convince myself to drink the warm beer and stay till the end of their set. The concert ended with a cover of an Irving Berlin tune, forgot the name. My sister texted me. She's at my mom's house tonight. They keep telling me to move back and give up on my art... But I know Los Angeles is where I belong. Don't forget the parable of the talents like my family did. Don't you make me make you remember, Illy? Oh yeah, how was your date????

I contemplated the repercussions of responding and decided not to, then Randolph Royce texted me.

Did you bang her?

Chapter Seven

Rachel: Belle

All a Belle wants is her Beast. A Beast can be either a man who fought for success to the point of receiving disfiguring amounts of emotional and psychological scarring or an ugly or large man that might scare people at first but actually has a tender heart. A Belle would do anything for her Beast, would maul and kill for him. The thought of being held in those big arms and dwarfed by a giant body is simply too all-consuming. The real Beast is inside Belle.

As for her own personality traits, Belles are hyper intelligent and use that intelligence to fantasize constantly. They fall in love with books as hard as they do with people. They develop attachment and dependency issues with men. It takes a certain kind of man to father a Belle, one that lets her know she's a princess no matter the size of their castle. Belles deserve love, they don't earn it.

~ * ~

Did you bang her?
I let Royce's text linger.
No, I replied.
Why the hell not? I made sure to throw you the easiest girl first.
Not my type.
Too feminine?
No...look, let me pick where I take the next girl. I have to do this my way. I can't pretend.
You're a private eye, of course you can.
Work's different.

Fine, where do you want to take her?

Somewhere simple, a bar.

Done, the owner of Rochelle's off of Wilshire is my Godfather's son. He's got a great place.

I was thinking more like Johnny's bar.

Where's that?

Down the street.

You won't impress anyone taking them there.

Not trying to.

Fine, I'll call ahead and start a tab. All your drinks are on me.

Thanks.

Just don't fuck this up or these girls will start getting pissed at me for passing them to a guy that passes on them.

I won't.

I wasn't trying to impress anyone, I was trying to find David York's killer, and if I could get a few drinks with a beautiful girl to get my detective wheels turning at the same time, then lucky me. This time I didn't pick her up, I had her meet me at the bar.

Johnny's was a small place, more of a bunker than a dive. Owner operated so smoking cigarettes inside was grandfathered in by law. I lit up the moment. The bartender was a beautiful red head outlaw cowgirl, covered from her neck down in tattoos and wearing a Stetson. There was a pool table, TV, and jukebox and with those three items, it was a surprise that the place was ever dead. Which tonight, it definitely was. It was just the bartender, an old man hocking up a lung in the back, and me. I sat at the bar.

"You must be Royce's guy," the bartender said.

"That's me."

"Where's the chick?"

"On her way."

"Need a drink while you wait?"

"Jameson double on the rocks."

She poured me a triple.

"Pace yourself," she winked.

"What's a guy working with the likes of Randolph Royce doing in a crumby place like this?"

"Looking for information. What do you know about a man named David York?"

"The fat lawyer?"

"Yeah."

"Used to drink Jameson, too, except wasn't a fan of rocks."

"That's it? Wasn't he a regular?"

"He came here once a week but kept to himself, mostly. He didn't like to make small talk...or even courteous talk."

"That's strange...I always took him for an angry drunk."

"He always seemed about to explode...always looked a little pink."

"You have to know more than that."

"He was better acquainted with the owner."

"Who's that?"

"Johnny, *duh*."

"Can you give me his number?"

"Nope, your only chance to talk to him is coming in at the right time."

"When would the right time be?"

"Once every blue moon."

"How's the moon looking tonight?"

"Haven't checked."

The corral style doors swung open and in walked my date, dressed in princess yellow. She was the winner of a genetic lottery. Tall with long arms, legs, and fingers like me but for some reason, we consider what she has beauty and what I have disorder.

"You're ravishing," I complimented her.

"Thank you and you're winsome," she replied and sat on the barstool next to mine then spun around on it making three revolutions. "This place was a great choice."

I smiled and the bartender crept over.

"You thirsty?"

"Make me something pink."

The bartender grabbed a bunch of upper shelf bottles and whipped together a cosmopolitan.

"What's your name?"

"Rachel and you are?"

"Illy."

"Wow, I like that name...I've never dated an Illy."

"Ever date any Randolphs?"

"He took me to dinner a couple of times...he said that you were completely different though and I can see what he means...and I like what I see."

I blushed, "I like what I see too."

"Everyone likes seeing me."

Her cosmopolitan arrived and she slammed it down in four gulps until all that was left were a few pink, pulpy drops at the bottom of the martini glass.

"I need to go to the bathroom. I'll take another though." She pushed back off of the barstool and floated over to the bathroom, leaving the bartender, the old man hocking up his lung, and me alone.

"What a woman...*achock*," muttered the old man.

"What do you think?" I asked the bartender.

"A dime a dame."

"What do you mean?"

"*A Dime a Dame* by Barry Winslow and the Breezes was David York's favorite song to play on that jukebox. Every time he came in, the first thing he'd do was put in a dollar and play that song."

I slid off of my barstool and walked over to the jukebox. I pushed the flip button left until it arrived on the "B" page for Barry Winslow. The song's number was B44...the Ticking Man's tip. He must've known that I was on the York case, that David York listened to this song at this bar and that I would come to this bar. How the Ticking Man came to know all that was so troubling to ponder that I put in my dollar and played the song just so my mind could wander elsewhere.

A dime a dame
But I only have a nickel
What to do in such a pickle?
Find a dame that ain't so fickle
A dime a dame

But I only have a penny
If I pinch it I make twenty
That'll get me two dames
Both of them named Jenny
But one for me is plenty
Because I'm only looking for one love

"Isn't it a nice little song?" the bartender was on the verge of swooning.

I strolled back to the bar.

"The guy was a hopeless romantic with the heart of an old-school misogynist."

"I've never met a man that wasn't a misogynist. In fact, the phony feminists are the worst ones."

"I don't think so, I love women." I wondered what Disney princess I would classify the bartender as...perhaps Ariel...*yeah, definitely*.

A big budget boxing promo for the annual big fight appeared on the TV. I sat back down at the bar to watch it.

In just one week the score will be settled! Street Kid Spencer Casey will challenge featherweight champion Dapper Danny Brown only on Pay Per View. Don't miss one for the history books.

Professional fighting, whether boxing or mixed martial arts had become a form of proxy class war. Always the poor versus the rich and always the rich taking home the gold, but still the poor never lost hope.

"My money's on Dapper Danny," the bartender informed me.

"Why do you say that? Spencer's got a better right and record."

"Because Spencer's going to take a dive. You never bet on the poor fighter on the first fight. He won't win until after he gets his pay day and rebrands himself."

"Never count a poor boy out. If he's really from the streets, no amount of money would be sweeter than knocking out those rich white teeth."

Rachel came out the women's bathroom and I could hear the sound of the toilet flushing follow her out of the door. She sat back down next to me the moment her second cosmopolitan was finished.

"Did you see the man with the black glasses?" she asked then slammed down her drink.

"No, where?"

She pointed to a clock on the wall that had a drawing of the Ticking Man. His hands told the minute and hour while a thin third arm stretched out from his crotch to point out the second.

"Busy little member he's got," she laughed.

I followed suit, laughing with her, sounding natural.

"Do you read?" she asked.

"Too much."

"What was the last book you read?"

"Black Money, Ross Macdonald."

"He's good but he never had Chandler or Hammett's swagger."

"Macdonald made up for swagger with richer mystery. Speaking of Chandler and Hammett though, are you more of a Sam Spade or Philip Marlowe type of gal?"

"I don't mind either as long as Bogart's in the role,. but if I had to choose...Marlowe."

I jeered, so offended by her taste in actors that every muscle in my face seemed to cramp up in disgust.

"You mean to tell me you think Bogie was a better Marlowe than Elliot Gould?"

"Course he was. Altman didn't do Chandler...Altman did Altman."

"Altman's take was more Chandler than any other Chandler flick ever. Marlowe wasn't suave, Marlowe was eccentric."

"Like you?"

"If you see so."

"You ever been to jail?"

I laughed, "Once."

"For what?"

"Two years ago, I was on a plane heading back to Los Angeles from New York..."

"How did you like New York?"

"They didn't let me past the gate."

She laughed.

"I was flying back to LA and we hit some turbulence, you know standard bad weather...or so we thought. Turns out it was the storm of the century we were flying through. Suddenly, the plane started to plummet...people were screaming, crying, praying, the oxygen masks fell out the ceiling, so you know what I did?"

"What?"

I lit my second smoke of the date, "I lit a smoke."

Rachel laughed her ass off, slapping her knee, pounding the bar.

"Then what happened?"

"We made an emergency landing in Oklahoma City airport where the cops were waiting for me on the strip."

"They took you to jail for smoking?"

"It was a menthol."

She was hollering, hysterical with hilarity, tears steaming.

"Holy shit..." She wiped her tears with a napkin, still chuckling a bit.

I finished my Jameson and felt the water works backing up my pipes, "I'm going to the bathroom, be right back."

"Alright."

I strolled over to the men's room and walked over to the last urinal in the row. I unzipped, whipped it out, and took a long, relieving leak. My eyes rolled to the back of my head and crossed on the inside. It felt like I could go on forever.

I heard the door open behind me and a large figure stepped up to the urinal next to mine. His presence shut off my bladder, like a clogged-up faucet. I looked over and it was Mr. Tick Tock himself.

"Take a look, I don't mind," the Ticking Man smirked.

"What? No...are you following me?"

"If you don't take a look, you'll never know how much bigger than you I am. You need to know not to mess with me, kid."

I took a deep sigh and my eyes strayed over to their corners. *It* was monstrous.

"What's your problem, man? Why are you here!?"

"I'm helping you, ass-hole."

"Really?"

"The sixth pin."

"What?"

Just like that, the Ticking Man finished pissing, zipped up, and walked out, leaving me high and dry to listen to his toilet flush itself.

"You forgot to wash your hands," I shouted at him as he left.

The sixth pin, what could he mean? As my mind tried to wrap itself around this new clue, I started pissing again, heaving out another minute's worth of waste. I finished, shook myself off, zipped up, flushed, washed my hands with soap, dried them off, then left the bathroom.

When I returned to the bar, the tender was the only female present.

"What happened? Where'd she go?" I asked.

"Left with the owner."

"What?"

"Yeah, the big guy with the black glasses, that's Johnny. He swooped in on her while you were in the john. No pun intended."

"Unbelievable... just my luck."

"She left you a note."

The bartender handed me a white napkin with blue ink scribbles. The note read as follows:

Illy, I think you're a swell guy but you're just not my beast. That said, if it wasn't for you, I wouldn't have met the man who I think is my soul mate. At first, I thought it could be you, I even imagined some complicated movie set scenario where we were both actors in a musical with you going off script to sing your proposal to me. Now I know Johnny is the only one for me. I'm sorry but I hope you can find it in your heart to feel happy for me. Thank you so much.

I stepped out of the bar and saw the Ticking Man and Rachel peel out of a parking spot in a black Dodge. His arm was already over her shoulder as he drove the car himself.

The bartender stepped out for a moment and firmly stroked the mane of my neck to console me.

"I'm sorry, dear."

"It's okay. Tell me, does the sixth pin mean anything to you?"

"That ol' failed strip club bowling alley experiment off Sixth and San Pedro?"

I drove through Highland Park to old downtown where Skid Row used to be. It looked like a ghost town built on top of the sacred Indian burial site of the white capitalist dream. Ten years ago, they gentrified the area, displaced all the bums, and built a bunch of bourgeois shops that no one ever bought a thing from. I parked at the corner where David York's body once laid. There were no gifts, flowers, or candles, nothing to commemorate him. I put my hand on the concrete and felt the strange friction of painful memories against my skin. Across the street was what used to be The Sixth Pin, decadence's tomb. Vagrants had spray-painted all sorts of symbols and wailing faces on the building. I checked around the back and saw three words written on the wall, EAT THE RICH.

~ * ~

Homicide Report for Rachel Sayles by Vic Spinoza
6-23-25
Rachel Sayles' body was found in pieces around the county junkyard. Murderer left her eyeball in the office's mail shoot so they would call the police and investigate. Her legs were found in a junk car's trunk, her head in a broken refrigerator, and her arms on a heap of stinking garbage. Her abdomen has yet to be recovered but if they wanted us to find it, we would've. Bite marks and animal hairs were all over her body. Hair samples are still at the lab to confirm the creature's species but we suspect they're from a canine variety, some breed of dog, wolf, or dingo. No foot or fingerprints found at the scene.

~ * ~

I parked outside my apartment complex and stayed in the driver's seat, smoking, deducing. Eat the Rich...Rawr...Rr...graffiti...Rocky Rude? Perhaps, but why and to what capacity? The Ticking Man was trying to point me in the right direction.

Carino texted me.

How's it hanging, Gnomeo? I had a strange dream last night. I dreamt that mankind dealt so much damage to the Earth even the forces of destiny could no longer act properly upon it, leaving people to chase dreams that should be fulfilled but never are, even if their dreams meet destiny's criteria. Imagine that, destiny relying on environmental conditions... I came by your spot earlier, just wanted to check it out. Sometimes I do that, I guess I just get bored. I saw your ex chillin' in a car nearby. She didn't recognize me. She never met me, right? She was with someone, blonde dude. Looked like they were waiting for someone. Looked pissed. After that I crept over to the old Dodger's stadium. Found a chill spot in the catacombs. I'll take you some time, it's a good place to take a broad. You can bring the one you took to Johnny's. Who do you have on the big fight? My moneys on Dapper Danny.

I finished my cigarette and flicked it into the street. Out of nowhere, Maria reached in through the passenger's side window, pulled up the door lock, and hopped in next to me.

"Have you come up with any leads?"

"Still working on it...the big picture's getting clearer."

"I know you went to the scene of the crime?"

"That means I got at least two people following me."

"I'm not one of them."

"I can smell him on you, that cheap cologne."

"I don't know what you're talking about."

"Sure, you don't...it's fine, I don't care, just tell him to keep a distance."

"Right now, this case is your priority, not your high-class whores."

Maria sneered at me then exited my car, slamming the door.

"Bye," I gave her the peace the sign but she didn't look back.

Chapter Eight

Calpurnia: Cinderella

I can't sleep, not because of what's lurking in my dreams but because of what's stirring in my apartment. The lights are off and I unplugged all the electronics, but there's still this unsettling room tone. The pipes drone and the floors creak and the walls whimper and the ghosts murmur but there's this feeling of closing in and that makes the heavy sound of miniscule amounts of air slowly being displaced. I turn my phone on to distract my mind. If I can't sleep, the screen will supplement my dreams. I see a few texts from Randolph Royce, the first one berating me about my poor skills with women, the second informing me of my third date, and the following six wondering why I haven't responded yet and demanding that I do.

It won't happen again, I promise you...I will score with the next one.

You freakin' better.
Can I choose where to take her again?
Where?
I can't say...it's a secret.
You won't tell me?
It's that underground.
Fine, I don't think I want to know.
I'll pick her up, what's her address?
5424 Newcastle Avenue, Encino, CA, 91316
A valley girl?
That's right, still lives with her parents.

I took the day leading up to the date to make a chart of suspects and information I've gathered in David York's murder case.

Suspects:

Jonny/The Ticking Man—Followed me on both dates, he was either hired by Randolph Royce or Maria to tail me. B44 and the Sixth Pin were his tips to me before he stole both of my dates.

Rocky Rude—Considers me her muse and may spray paint under the pen name 'Rawr'. Rocky Rude was at the solstice party, so perhaps she has a connection to Randolph Royce other than having the same initials.

Maria—Had a multitude of marital problems then came to her ex-husband to investigate. She might be trying to trap me with Spinoza's aid.

Clues:

Pacifica cigar found in David York's esophagus.

A Dime a Dame by Barry Winslow and the Breezes.

Jameson whiskey, straight.

The Sixth Pin.

Looking through the folder Maria gave me, I found three potential suspects who held grudges with York after unsavory divorce settlements. The first was a Muay Thai kick boxer named Eric Wang, the second was the owner of the Bulldozer beer brewery named Pablo Perkins, and the third was a name I recognized; the homeless man with the burned face, Monty Freed.

I zipped out of the house and checked out the Bengal Tiger Kickboxing Club where Eric Wang trained and taught. Here's the perk of looking different, people might see you and know you don't belong but wouldn't dare say anything. I stepped into the grimy gym and walked over to the ring where Eric Wang was sparring a man two weight classes above him. Eric bobbed and weaved away from every slow battering ram punch and kick until seizing his opportune moment to drive a knee into his opponent's stomach and knock every ounce of wind out of him. Once he dropped the guy, Eric walked back to his corner, so I hopped onto the ring apron and got into his ear.

"Eric Wang?"

"Yes?"

"I'm a private detective investigating the murder of David York..."

"York is dead?"

"As a door knob."

"Oh, my god..."

"I'm sorry."

"Fuck yea. This is amazing. I love you, man," with every celebratory remark he swiped a fist through the air.

"I know Mr. York burned you, so let it all out, I won't judge."

"Woo. Yes. Yes. Yes." He did a little dance, raising his hands like he had just won the championship belt and confetti was raining down from the ceiling.

"Will you answer a few questions about your relationship with him?"

"Sure thing, do you mind if we talk outside?"

"Fine."

Wang hopped out of the ring and threw a towel over his head to dry off. He quickly hustled outside the gym as I followed him to a tree. The tree was the height of two men and the thickness of a single meaty one. Eric Wang threw his towel off and got into fighting stance in front of the tree.

"What did you want to ask me?"

"Did you kill David York?"

Smiling, he focused all his strength in his leg and shrieked.

"Aaaaayaaaah," like a war cry.

With each thunderous kick that Eric Wang sent into the tree, he let out a different word.

"If. I. Killed. David. York. I. Would've. Bragged. About. It. To. The. Whole. World."

By the time his sentence was finished and he delivered his last kick, the tree's body was hacked away into a single thread of tissue that snapped, making the tree tip over to the ground. Eric Wang's shin was bleeding profusely and covered with wounds and splinters.

"David York was an evil man. He kicked wounded men while they were down. He deserved to die, but I didn't kill him."

I knew he was telling the truth because had he killed York, he would've used his bare hands and feet.

Pablo Perkins owned Bulldozer Beer brewery up in Sun Valley and

I didn't mind doing some day-drinking before I grabbed lunch with Carino. I checked in with one of the tour groups that would be guided through the brewery. Once the rest of the tour was being taken to the gift shop, I snuck in between two large metal tanks to do my own snooping. I could hear a faint singing coming from far away. *"A dime a dame, but I only have a nickel, what to do in such a pickle?"*

With every line of lyric, I drew closer to the source until I snuck up to an office door and clung to the wall outside. After I heard a hiccup, I felt strolling right in would do no harm.

Pablo Perkins was sitting at his desk, surrounded by empty beer bottles and polishing off another to add to the pile.

"Hey. *Hic*. You. *Hic*. What are you doing in here?" he shouted at me.

"Took the tour, liked what I saw, and wanted to sample the product."

"We have a bar."

"They don't offer the private stash."

He looked at me for a moment, gauging me, till one pupil wandered away in a drunken stupor then rolled around on the belly of his eye.

"You got some balls...here."

He knelt down and picked up two stone cold Bulldozer Blueberry Ale bottles and threw one to me. I popped it open with my lighter and raised it to him.

"To the death of David York."

"To the death of David York," he repeated.

I took a long suckle at the bottle, as did Pablo.

"So, you knew?"

"Course I did. David was a friend."

"Even though he helped your ex-wife take your home and half your worth?"

"He was doing his job and I had it coming. Gotta respect a man that's good at what he does. Turned out he was good at plenty more than divorces."

"Why'd you have it coming? Because you were a drunk?"

He laughed, hiccupping between ha's.

"No. Because I was sober...too stiff. I needed to loosen up. My wife used to drink me under the table then whip me in the sack."

"Who do you think killed David York?"

"It was a suicide, one hundred percent."

"Yeah right, you should see the pictures of the scene."

"All I know is David wanted death like a baby wants its bottle. He's in a better place now even if that's nowhere."

"Why would he want to die?"

"A toxic cocktail of love, spoiled rotten and being hated by the whole world. Money isn't everything in this life...how we earn it matters."

Pablo polished off his beer while I was only a few inches deep into mine.

"You going to finish that?"

I passed him the bottle and he tipped it to me.

"Thanks," he said then finished that too.

I figured Pablo Perkins was clean, the only tip I could get out of the guy was how to beat a hangover. His solution was a raw quail egg with two drops of Tabasco.

Carino and I decided to meet up in Highland Park for lunch off the corner of 59th avenue and Figueroa. He got a pork torta and used an extra meal coupon to get me four beef tongue tacos. We spoke while chewing.

"Where would I find Monty Freed?"

"Who?"

"Homeless guy with the burned face."

"Oh, we call him Monty Burns, like from The Simpsons."

"Where does he stay?"

"Not in any one spot. Your best bet to find him is by coming tonight."

"I was planning on it. I'm bringing a date."

"Cool, just make sure she's not a snitch."

"I'll be able to tell the moment I meet her. if she fails the test, you won't be seeing her."

~ * ~

Robert Shepyer

The sun had set and the night's humidity soared. I drove over to my date's parent's house where I could hear the hellacious screaming of a married couple that wanted each other dead. My date snuck out through the front door, wearing a pearl blue dress and heels. She closed the door ever so silently before tip-toeing to my car, opening the car door, and sitting down. She closed the door so slowly that you could only hear the click.

"Evenin' miss."

She put her finger to her lips, "*Shhhhh...*" and pointed forward.

I drove off quietly until she broke the silence at the end of the block.

"Thank God, I needed to get out of that hell hole so bad."

"Glad that I could help."

"Thanks, I'm Calpurnia."

"I'm Illy, nice to meet you."

"Where are you taking me, Illy?"

"Somewhere so special and secret you can never talk about it to anyone but me, okay?"

"Okay."

"Promise?"

"This sounds creepy."

"I swear it's not, it's beautiful."

"Okay, I trust you...promise."

"Awesome, I hope you like to dance."

I took her to the abandoned subway station in what used to be Pershing Square. In Los Angeles, more mobility has always meant more power, ever since Ford closed down the original subway system to foster freeway culture. The subways were once a hub for the poor to preach and plot against the rich, so when the fallout of the great shift divided the classes, the rich closed down the subways, forcing the poor to stay powerless, in one place. At the boarded-up entrance, there was a single hole in a wooden plank where I could see a guard's eye watching us.

"What's the password?"

"Eat the rich," I replied.

He shifted the wooden planks to create a doorway for us to enter and once we did, we could hear swing music echoing up from the bottom level.

"Wow, I can't believe something like this really exists."

"Take my hand, let's not waste any time."

She put her hand in mine and together we ran down a dormant escalator to the bottom floor where we saw the party of the century well underway. Speakeasy swing in stadium numbers, the poor had congregated here from every corner of the county. The house band was blowing their horns till their faces turned blue. Poor men were tossing up poor women and catching them, straight and gay couples of every color were swinging in each other's arms. Love and lust were in the underground air.

"I'm not really sure if I know how to swing."

"It's easy, just follow my lead."

The basics of swing dancing are comprised of four steps and though our dancing wasn't the most eye-catching, Calpurnia's beauty made us the center of attention. Side to side, back and forth, we did our best to show off, maybe throwing in a dip from time to time.

Once the band wrapped up the song and we were both sweating buckets, I noticed Monty Freed standing at the edge of the party, hands in pockets, staring at his feet.

"See that guy over there?" I asked Calpurnia.

She took a look Monty's way and dashed over to him without answering me.

When a set of heels appeared in the view of his two feet, Monty looked up in disbelief that such a beauty paid him mind.

"May I have this dance?" Calpurnia asked.

"Of course," Monty mumbled, shaken.

She took his hands and they began to dance, her cheek against the unburned side of his face. Suddenly, the entire party stopped dancing to watch them and Carino began a contagious applause that took hold of the entire party. It became Monty's moment. Tears streamed down his face and Calpurnia began wiping them away.

"It's alright...this isn't really you."

"Thank you."

What princess was Calpurnia? I don't know, maybe they ought to make one based on her because Calpurnia was acting as selfless as the Princess Diana of Disney. Once the song was over, I walked over to Monty, clapping for him.

"Wow, with moves like that you're going to make me look bad."

"Oh, I'm sorry, I didn't mean nothing by it..."

"I'm just kidding, Monty. You were great... listen there's something I wanted to talk to you about."

Another song began and Calpurnia found a new dance partner. I took the opportunity to pull Monty away for the party to pick his brain.

"Do you know a man named David York?"

He shriveled up with fear, like I had pointed a gun in his face, "Oh no...not him...please tell me he didn't ask for me."

"He's dead."

"Phew," the stress melted off of his face.

"What did he do to you?"

"He settled my divorce and after I lost everything, he offered me work for some friends of his. One of those friends introduced me to the guy that did this to me," pointing to the burned side of his face.

"Yeah and which friend was that?"

"This billionaire real estate tycoon named Randolph Royce."

For a moment, I was deafened to the party and was watching a phantasmagoria of everything leading up to this moment.

"What's wrong? You know him?"

"The guy who burned your face, what was his name?"

"Big fella named Dante."

"Thanks a lot, Monty. You made my job painfully easy."

I split without so much as a goodbye then made my way to Calpurnia who was in a veteran dancer's arms. When he whipped her out and her hand thrust back, I was there to grab it and pull her away.

"Hey, we're in the middle of something," the dancer exploded.

"Tough," I replied as I rushed Calpurnia away. "We're leaving," I told her.

"To where?"

"Somewhere quiet."

We fled from the subway back to my car where I was too lost in my own thoughts to make conversation.

"I really like where you took me, Illy."

"No problem."

"I really like you too."

"Thanks."

"I have to be home by midnight, but until then what do you say we check out your place?"

"Fine."

I drove us to my apartment, totally indifferent to what she would think of the mess. It was dirty and stinking and covered with old clothes and trash. When she opened the door and beheld the apartment, all she could probably think of was what it would look like clean.

"Do you have a vacuum?"

"Yea, why?"

Right then and there, in the middle of the room, she stripped down to her underwear and opened up a closet to hang her dress.

"I am going to clean this place up for you."

"You don't have to, really it's no problem."

"No, I need to. I'm a neat-freak, all I do all day is clean my house, so when I see a mess like this, if I don't clean it then I'll feel dirty."

"Alright, do what you have to do."

I walked over to the kitchen and opened the fridge. Inside there was nothing but a single can of beer, butter, bread, and salt. I took out the beer and popped it open then sat on my couch to sip it and watch her clean.

While she was bent over and picking up my dirty drawers in her clean ones, I realized which princess Calpurnia was. Raised in a broken home with a talent for housekeeping and midnight curfew, she fit the glass slipper for the Cinderella role perfectly. She picked up, folded and hung all my clothes. She vacuumed my floors, dusted my shelves, washed my windows, and organized my papers. She picked up David York's case folder and showed it to me.

"Where should I put this?"

"Just leave it on my desk."

Suddenly, a teeny, tiny, slim piece of metal slipped out of the folder and onto the floor. I jerked my neck forward in curiosity then launched myself out of my chair to grab it. I took a good look at it, examining each dimension.

"What is it?"

"It's a recorder." I realized.

Maria was setting me up...but why? Revenge?

"Calpurnia, do you need me to take you home?"

"What time is it?"

I checked my wristwatch and it read eleven forty-five p.m.

"Eleven forty-five."

"Oh no..."

She dashed to the closet and retrieved her pearl dress than slipped it on within seconds.

"Can I order you a ride?" I tried to ask her but she was already out the door and running out of the complex.

I walked out onto my balcony and saw her running up the street so hard, she lost her pearl heel and just kept going. Moments later, the Ticking Man was walking up the street, found the slipper then pocketed it.

I lit a smoke and took a long drag, but before I could exhale, four armored cop cars rushed up to my apartment complex's entrance and spilled out their humans. One of which was Detective Vic Spinoza, smoking too...in the same breathing rhythm as me, it seemed.

"Illy Robin, you're under arrest for suspicion in the murders of Millie Glupnick and Rachel Sayles. We have a search warrant. Please surrender peacefully."

"Is this a prank? Am I on TV? I know you're recording me."

"Both girls wound up in body bags after dating you, Robin. I know all about how you treat women. It's time I put an end to your mean streak."

"Hang on, let me get my attorney on the line," I took my phone out of my pocket and starting dialing Dieter Rumbledorfer's number.

The police began banging at my door while Spinoza smoked his cigarette below my balcony.

"Better get that," he smirked.

I sighed, put my phone away, and opened the door to let the cops in to cuff me and take me away. I sat in the front seat of my own cop car, watching the city pass me by in choppy, streaks of light and colossal shadows.

Chapter Nine

Prisoner of Society

The universe always makes the first move, usually with a person acting on its behalf. If the universe tries to harmonize with you and you resist it, if you're surrounded by love but always mistake it for fear, if everywhere you look you see hopeless omens...don't be surprised if you end up in a cell if not dead. Love is inevitable so long as you accept it.

I was sitting in a chair, alone and trying to find some imperfection in the room to focus in on and distract myself with. There wasn't a crack or stain or tile out of place but Millie and Rachel were dead so any sense of order was only an illusion. I juggled the potential suspects, including some split personality version of myself that howled out of me at the sight of the moon...but still, I wouldn't put it past Spinoza to frame me by hiring a hitman to follow me and kill off my dates. The room was totally silent until Vic opened the door. His shoes had felt on their soles to not make a sound when they treaded. This was an old sensory deprivation tactic used in Russian prisons to break inmates.

"You have to find Johnny, the owner of Johnny's bar," I stammered at Spinoza.

"Shut up, you'll speak when spoken to."

I shrugged and submitted to what would be the most unusual of punishments.

"Who said you could sit down?"

"No one, there was a chair so I figured..."

"Stand up and stay up, we got eyes on you," Spinoza pointed to an orb in the ceiling. "If I see you sitting in that chair again, I'll throw you in the hole with the savages."

I stood up from the chair.

"You can play the blame game all you want, but I know it was you. I had a sneaking suspicion that you were capable of this kind of depravity since high school. A mug like yours has to be up to no good. We'll begin the interrogation as soon as my partner is ready, so just stand there and wait."

Spinoza silently stepped out and I gazed up at the eye in the sky on the ceiling. How long had I been under their microscope? What could they blackmail me with?

The door opened again, only this time it was a beautiful brunette also wearing felt soled shoes.

"Illy Robin, my name is Detective Lisa Holt, I'm Vic's partner in this case...who gave you permission to stand?"

"Detective Spinoza..."

"A standing prisoner is a plotting prisoner, get in the fucking chair. There's a reason it's there."

I sighed and sat back down.

"What you did to those poor, innocent girls is fucking disgusting and justice for them will be reaped upon you, Mr. Robin. I'm going to make sure they tie you to the stake and burn you alive."

"It wasn't me...I have an alibi. Ask Johnny, the owner of Johnny's bar."

"Listen, Illy, I don't know what kind of tab you got racked up over there but don't throw an innocent man under the bus. This will all be easier as soon as you confess...now sit in that chair and wait."

She strode out as I hung my head. I heard the door open and looked up to see Spinoza again.

"What the fuck did I say about sitting down?"

He stormed over, lifted me up by the collar then threw me against the wall.

"I'm sorry, Detective Holt told me..."

"Don't you filthy up that angel's name in your dirty mouth."

I nodded and he got in so close, his nose was nearly touching mine.

"Your ex-wife has got a really nice set of legs, Robin. How the hell did you ever land a prize like her?"

"I don't know."

"Well, you better figure that out and tell me, because I'm taking her out this weekend and I need tips."

"She likes cartoons, especially Disney."

"Then I guess I should take her to Disneyland, shouldn't I?"

"Good idea, she likes the tea cups."

"Say, you don't think it's weird that I want the girl you already had, do you?"

"No. Not weird at all."

"You lying to me, Robin?"

"Sex is not subtractive. No one comes out with less."

"Unless you like to bite," Spinoza clicked his teeth together then let me go and slithered out the door.

"Fuck me," I said to myself as I closed my eyes, pulled my head back, and banged it against the wall.

"What? How dare you?"

I opened my eyes to find Detective Holt standing there.

"Again with the standing?"

Detective Holt rushed over and grabbed my balls in a stiff wrenching grasp.

"I am not a piece of ass, Mr. Robin. I am a piece of shit for how I treat prisoners."

She twisted her grip and sent an awkward rush of pain through my body.

"SoRry, sOrry, SorrY!"

"Sit down. NOW."

She released me and I slowly sat down, having to cup my junk as my butt planted on the seat. Looming over me, Holt crossed her arms over her chest and curled her lip.

"We could really use you around here, ya know?"

"What do you mean?"

"The state's in need of prisoners to experiment new rehabilitation programs on. I think you'd be a great guinea pig."

Just then, the door opened and Spinoza joined us.

"Sitting down again? Do you take me for a jackass, Illy?"

I stood up.

"Did he ask you to stand?" Detective Holt asked.

I sat back down.

"Did I ask you to sit?" Detective Holt shouted.

"Just fuckin' kill me, please," I wailed.

They ogled at me in my humiliated confusion and couldn't help but crack up.

"You haven't changed one bit since high school, Robin," Spinoza hollered, laughing.

I rolled my eyes and shook my head.

"I want my lawyer."

They both hushed up.

"That won't be necessary, your story checks out. A guy came with evidence that supports your alibi."

"If it wasn't you, my next guess is that after their dates the girls just off'd themselves." Detective Holt joked.

Spinoza laughed, shaking his head, "Too soon..."

"Who came to my rescue?"

"Your pal, Johnny."

I thought he misspoke, but when he escorted me out of the holding room, I saw the Ticking Man waiting for me in the lobby.

"What did you tell them?" I asked him.

"I didn't tell them anything, it's what I showed them."

"You have video of me?"

"Hours upon days upon weeks of it."

"Why?"

"Come with me," he strolled out the station's sliding doors and I followed him to his car where he threw me a blindfold. "Put this on, you can't know where I'm taking you."

I put on the blindfold, got in the car, and we traveled through the dark night of my soul.

Chapter Ten

The Overseeing Voyeur

My blindfold was lifted while I was sitting at a table in a backroom kitchen across from a boy who couldn't have been older than fifteen. His blonde hair fell mysteriously over his eyes and their black bags. I could sense this boy was severely disturbed.

"Illy Robin, case number two."

"Out of?"

"One hundred."

"One hundred what?"

"Test subjects."

"You call this a test?"

"That you've been failing terribly."

"How would you know?"

"I'm the O.V. which stands for Overseeing Voyeur but you can call me Ovid."

"What's an O.V. do, Ovid?"

"I watch thousands of hours of surveillance video."

"On me?"

"On all one hundred subjects."

"Do they all know someone is watching them?"

"Absolutely not, they would ask too many questions."

"You think I won't ask questions?"

"You will. I will have to live with the consequences of the answers, but unlike the other subjects, women aren't dying wherever they go... It doesn't take a detective to deduce more will die soon."

"If you're watching those girls, then you ought to know who's killing them."

"I do but I can't tell you."

I grabbed him by the collar, this limp little child that I could crumple in my fist if I wanted to. He didn't squirm or flinch; he wasn't afraid I'd hurt him. Maybe because he could see the future along with everything else and knew I only intended to scare him. He rolled his eyes at me, unafraid.

"Why?" I said through clenched teeth.

"Because that would interfere with our test and the test's integrity is my top priority. Solving this case for you would be cheating."

"As your subject, isn't my well-being of greater concern?"

"I guess we just have to bet on you surviving this."

"We?"

The Ticking Man entered the room and stood beside Ovid. I paused to stare at them and take in their oxymoronic presence then turned back to Ovid to ask him another question.

"Why am I failing this test?"

He sighed and shook his head then put his hand on my cheek.

"You poor thing...because you think too much, you did with Maria, you did with your dead dates, you have to act...strike while the iron's hot and seize the moment...no more self-hatred, pity, or deceit. No more narcissism, laziness, or fear; no more complicity, complexity, or loneliness. No more death or darkness...only love and light. Reconnect. Now. Change. Adapt. Or die... Definitely stop labeling women as Disney characters like some kind of asshole."

"You can read my mind too?"

"I wouldn't have this job unless I knew my subjects better than they know themselves."

"If all that's why I'm failing, I can't be the only subject doing poorly."

"To be honest, they're all going to fail and I can understand why, *this is the android age,* but I have hope for you."

"Why me?"

"BECAUSE YOU'RE A PRIVATE EYE, DAMN IT! Now stand up, Johnny will escort you out."

I stood up and Johnny walked over to lead me out but I paused a moment.

"Will I be seeing you again?" I asked Ovid.

"Just stare down the camera eye."

Johnny led me out of the kitchen and through a door that led to Johnny's bar. The usual suspects were there; the old man coughing and the bartender. The Dapper Danny/Street Kid Spencer fight was on TV and just as I was about to exit, Street kid Spencer threw a bunk hook too short and got a stiff uppercut to the chin, knocking him out cold...or so he wanted us to believe.

That night when I got home, I searched the apartment inside out, ruining all the sprucing up that Calpurnia worked so hard on. By the end of my search, I came up with thirty audio and video recording devices that had been placed in every tiny crevice of my apartment. Once I threw them all out, that room tone that had been bothering me was gone and I could finally sleep.

Chapter Eleven

Lucy: Jasmine

I woke up to a long string of texts from Carino.

Dude, you'll never believe what happened to me last night. After I cashed in my bet from the Dapper Danny brawl, I was cruising down Ventura boulevard with a six pack of Heineken looking for a shadowy spot on a side street to drink. My street senses tingled when I hit a cross-street called Cole, so I turned and walked until I found an even smaller street called Wagner. Walking down Wagner, my way lit only by the moon, I came upon a body. A girl with one pearl heel, her other foot was severed off. I wasn't sure if she was dead so I flipped her onto her back and saw two circular cuts where her tits used to be. Her eye sockets were open but the balls were missing and replaced with her own nipples. Breast milk tears. It was then that I realized this was your date, dead at my feet. I wanted to cry and run but...I had a six pack. I wasn't going to call the cops, so here I am texting you.

Was I supposed to call Spinoza? For all I know, he can see Carino's texts too. Poor Cinderella, by midnight the spell of life waned away. Then Royce texted me.

Your date tonight is a sure thing, rich girl that hates the rich. Only wants a poor guy like you.

But I'm not poor.

You are in my book but don't worry, by the numbers she's not really rich, at least to me.

I could see Royce sitting back, smoking a Pacifica covered in York's blood. My relationship with him might've started as something fairly innocent but it had to steer itself into crime eventually, a guy like Royce is connected to every dirty deed that happens in the tragic kingdom.

I was just a moth attracted to the fire.

A notification popped up on my phone to remind me that Rocky Rude's art show was tonight so I started stressing when I realized I'd have to juggle my date and the woman who considered me her muse. Though Rocky never said she loved me, I know a muse is only a stone's throw away from a lover.

~ * ~

Lucia was French, but all the Angelinos would call her Lulu or Lula till she settled with Lucy. She wanted to marry a Desi, short for Desiderio, but would settle for a Dez. She refused to let me pick her up so she ordered a car to my place and when she arrived, she forced me to let her drive my car. She held her cigarettes between her middle and ring fingers and it looked like she was giving me the ol' live long and prosper with every life shortening drag. We took the scenic route down the pacific coast highway and got to know each other.

"I'm just a rich bitch looking for my street rat."

"You're barking up the wrong tree, babe. I'm just an above average alley cat."

I had no problem throwing my chances for love away like trash if it didn't feel right, right out of the gate. Still, I always wanted a French friend and she always wanted a crippled friend.

"What's this art show we're going to?"

"Venice based painter named Rocky Rude, really good at portraits, said I was her muse."

"She must be a surrealist."

"You think she looks at me and sees tigers hatchin' out of eggs?"

"Something like that."

The coast, sky, and waves seemed to take on a surreal feel the more we talked about this girl. Even the concept of Rocky Rude had a certain stimulating and intoxicating element to it. As if the idea of her itself would dose you upon entering your brain. Lucy struggled not careening this car over the cliff's edge to our deaths.

"You ever see those Eat The Rich tags all over the poorer parts of town? Don't tell anyone but I think Rocky Rude is Rawr."

"Sure, I've seen them. I'm always around the poorer parts of town."

"Doing what?"

"Looking for a husband."

"Wouldn't your parents be upset?"

"I wouldn't tell them the truth. You see, French families play a game where we all lie to each other constantly and know it but pretend like it's the truth anyway."

"How do you beat the game?"

"When you lie enough to force someone into admitting the truth or into doing something they don't want to do for the sake of upholding the lie. For this you get twenty points...and you need two thousand to win."

"What's the reward for winning?"

"They start to believe you."

The sea breeze swept through Lucy's lush blonde locks as she drove us down the coast. She was so cool in this context, she could say anything and it would come out as art.

"I don't know why anyone chooses to make art these days...it's 2025, the best artist is an algorithm," she nodded to her own words with real style.

We arrived on the beach where the rich gathered by torchlight to celebrate the work of Rocky Rude. As soon as we got out of the car, Rocky ran up to me and pulled me by the arm.

"Illy, thank God you're here, I was about to leave."

"From your own show?"

Lucy followed us, indifferent. When I saw the collection Rocky put together for her show, I nearly vomited. I recognized the model in every painting. There was David York painted in acrylics, eyes shut and bleeding on the sidewalk as a Pacifica stuck out of his neck. There was Calpurnia in water color, eyes bleeding milk tears. There was Rachel, bitten to shreds and cut to pieces. There was a post-impressionist Millie, spine protruding out of her neck. There were the rich, drinking bubbly and strolling between the canvases murmuring words like "brilliant" and "genius" when all I thought was *suspect.*

"What do you think? Aren't you proud of me?" Rocky asked.

"Yeah, you really have a way with brushes."

Lucy crept up to my side and I whispered to her.

"We've got to get out of here."

"Why, we just arrived?" she asked.

"Who the fuck is this?" Rocky asked me, pointing at Lucy with her chin.

"Rocky, this is Lucy."

Just nodding at each other was enough to spark their epic hatreds.

"Listen...if I tell you that you're my muse, I don't want you bringing any strange chicks to my art shows."

"I'm sorry, I didn't know."

"It's alright, just tell your girl to watch her back."

Lucy just laughed, "Your art is fucking terrible."

"WHAT?" Rocky Rude blew a gasket.

"It's a trust fund baby impersonation act. The public will reject it no matter how much cash you pour into it."

"Who do you think you are?" Rocky Rude shrieked like a cancer-banshee.

"Your art should come with a label that says 'Not Real'," Lucy continued.

Rocky turned to me.

"Illy, I want her out of here, now."

"I'm sorry."

"NOW."

I grabbed Lucy by the arm and whisked her off of the beach and back to the car.

"You need to stay at my apartment tonight," I told Lucy.

"*WHAT?* You're a cool dude, don't get me wrong, but I like you as a friend and nothing more."

"It's not about sex, you're in danger now."

"Yeah right."

"You saw her art. All those portraits were of recent murder victims."

"She's not the killer."

"Yes, she is."

"No way, there's not a genuine thing about that chick. *Murder, that's genuine.*"

We arrived at the car, both by the driver's side.

"I'm driving," I informed her.

"Not while I'm in the car."

I sighed and handed her my keys.

She took us to her apartment, dropped herself off and I decided to stake out outside. It sure felt suspect being the only car on the road. I waited for hours but not a single shred of eeriness was aroused that night. Chain-smoking, the cherry of my cigarette seemed like nothing more than a firefly in the pitch-black night.

I took the longest, deepest, most painful drag of the night and found a gun pointed at my neck from a black leather glove extending into my window.

"Look straight. You look at me and you die." The voice had been modulated by some digitizing filter.

I did as he commanded but he pulled the trigger anyway. My cigarette went out and everything went black.

~ * ~

Homicide Report for Lucy Leroux by Vic Spinoza
6/28/25

The deceased was found in a dumpster belonging to and behind the Silverlake French restaurant Taix. Reeking of snails, she was naked and wrapped up in an Arabic carpet. When we rolled the corpse out, we discovered carved into her back, the words "Princess Jasmine." The Aladdin reference has no link to previous murders, perhaps this is by a different killer. No prints found on the carpet, body, or at the scene. No sign of sexual intercourse with victim.

Chapter Twelve

Sera: Mulan

Barabus beckoned the bribing beacon, the woeful sigil coursing blood. Death is the dissolving of the material world's thin veneer. The black triangle is all there ever was and is multiplying and tessellating into the white-shite sky. The burning incense of the behemoth's heart birthed the smoke that eddied up my nose and convinced my brain to alter my chemistry until I became the smoke itself. I trickled through the gates and traveled between graves until arriving at a tomb that read *Everybody wants to be the heartthrob of the mortuary.* I seeped through the tomb's seal and saw the bodies of the dead drinking the tears of the weeping tulip. Beyond them was my shrunken casket, open and waiting. I pooled myself inside then reanimated back into the Frankenstein.

~ * ~

I woke up in my bed, naked and with a strange object clenched in my limp left fist. I brought it to my eyes and saw it was a tranquilizer dart. I only now felt the dart's prick in my neck. I gripped it tight and shambled out of bed to the bathroom. I looked in the mirror and saw written in black marker on my chest *Lucy to*. What the gloved man meant was "Lucy too" because Lucy was dead. Whoever the gloved hand belonged to had either killed Lucy, was working with her killer, or didn't have anything to do with her killing. Perhaps the gloved man was being merciful, knocking me out to flush my mind of all the death and drama I swirled into. I was surprised by the absence of a headache. Instead, I felt rested and restored with newborn life-force. I looked at my phone and saw that it was ten thirty-seven a.m. The strange thing was that the date read July first. I had been asleep for three days. You'd expect me to have a long list of unanswered texts and missed calls with all that dead time but for some reason, no one bothered. My world slept with me.

I decided I would text Royce and break the silence.

Hey Randolph, when's my next date?

Illy?

Yeah.

I thought you were dead.

No...why would you think that?

An employee informed me.

Well, that was a lie.

Oh...I'll have to tell Sera the date's back on then.

I'm free tonight.

I'll let her know.

Whoever was killing off the beauties wanted to go out in a blood bath, so I might as well do him a solid and let Beretta James do what she does best and sing him to sleep with a bullet. I'd have to practice my aim until I could guarantee a shot between the eyes, into the brain. I hope my date finds the smell of gunpowder as seducing as I do.

I picked her up from her apartment in Inglewood, she was a beautiful, muscular dark chocolate amazon who strode like a cat down the concrete but had a black dragon tattoo running down her arm. Two cats in a cradle. I knew her and I could be. Black women always loved my company more authentically than white women. They loved how I talked and joked. Unlike white women, wanting to get laid wasn't on my mind as much as experiencing the pure joy of their company. She got in my car and the date began.

"Where are you taking me?"

"You ever shoot a gun before?"

"No, but I've always needed to."

"Good, today I'm going to teach you. What's your name, baby?

"Sera N. Dippity."

"Well dippity do da day."

We zoomed off to a firing range not too far from this cat's hideout.

"How do you know Randolph Royce?"

"I used to strip for him at the Sixth Pin, I'm still cashing checks he sends me to keep quiet about all the drugs and sex I saw...oops," she smiled devilishly.

"What a sweet deal. Have you ever tried blackmailing him?"

Her bombastic laugh shook me out of my nervousness.

"I like you, Illy...nah, I don't want to push my luck."

"I like you too, Sera. You're as real as they come."

I walked her into the firing range with my arm around her. We were splitting at the seams laughing, not letting other people carry on with their business. I rented her a Desert Eagle hand cannon knowing those amazon black dragon arms could handle the recoil. When asked what target posters we would like to shoot at, our options were bum, immigrant, terrorist, zombie, vampire, and custom upload.

"Custom upload? You mean I can take a picture and shoot at it?" Sera asked the clerk.

"Sure can, Miss," he answered while polishing a white revolver with his brown spit.

Quickly, she snapped a picture of me and handed her phone over to the clerk who sent the picture to the system to have a poster printed.

"Print two," she told the clerk.

"You want to shoot at me? Good luck, babe, I got nine lives."

"The mag comes with ten bullets."

"Better not miss twice."

"Bitch, the black dragon never does."

We printed two large posters of myself and brought them to the range where we hung them up and donned our ear-muffs. The first thing I showed her was how to load her mag by applying deliberate and precise strength to stuff up each bullet.

"How come you didn't rent yourself a gun?"

"I already got Beretta James."

I pulled Beretta James out from my leg holster and showed it to Sera.

"She looks special."

"You should see her shoot."

I raised Beretta James up and gazed down her back to the poster of me, aiming right between my eyes. I pulled her trigger and she birthed triplets, bullet after bullet after bullet.

Scat, scat, scat.

"How does she sound?"

"Beautiful, but it looks like you didn't hit anything."

I reeled the poster in and discovered it was completely unscathed.

"Just need some practice. Good P.I.s don't have to use their piece."

"Me next, I want to try."

Sera raised her gun to the poster, closed one eye and focused the other on my head.

"Here, let me help you," I got behind Sera and held her arms up and fixed her stance and aim.

"What do you think you're doing? With your help, I'll miss every shot."

I pulled my arms away and crossed them over my chest to just watch.

"Fine, you think you can do better? Prove it, black dragon."

She fired three rounds.

Head shot. Head shot. Head shot.

She reeled the poster in for us to study and I saw myself with bullet holes for pupils and a blazing third eye.

"Wow, perfect triangle," I admired.

"I'm a natural," Sera smiled.

"Now that I've warmed up, let me show you how it's done."

"Okay, okay...we gettin' cocky now, huh...? Well Mr. cocky, cock that shit and shoot."

I closed my eyes and meditated on my marksman's mantra. *Beretta James don't fail me now, let your black beauty soul aim that bullet true.* I pried my left eye open for sight and my third eye for clarity. I could see my target's soul materialize into one ethereal bubble begging to be burst to splatter its dream debris everywhere.

"Scat, scat, scat." my gun sang.

In tune but off target, again I hadn't made a single shot.

"It's a good thing you ain't a cop," Sera jabbed.

"You're damn right it is," I nodded.

Sera raised her weapon, ready to fire.

"Lock and load, cracka ass motha fucka."

Head shot. Head shot. Head shot. Head shot. Head shot. Head shot. Head shot.

She brought her gun's smoking barrel up to her cherry gloss lips and ever so gently, blew till the steel cooled, hardened and throbbed as if begging for more action.

"You never fuck with the black dragon."

"With skills like yours there's nothing I'd rather do than fuck the black dragon."

"Too bad marksmanship ain't sexually transmitted," she winked.

We drew closer to one another, pulled by the sheer magnetism of sexualized violence. As our lips came closer together, her gun's barrel perched right under my chin.

"If I miss you get a kiss."

"Fire away."

Her finger quivered at the trigger, but she knew just as well as I did that she could put me out of my misery with just one…

Click.

…Kiss.

Her mag was empty. I earned that kiss. My lips lurched toward hers, now only the slim width of a bullet away. The door opened and we had company, so Sera pulled back.

"Whatchu doin', crazy white-boy? I ain't tryin' to fuck wit' you," she shouted at me, looking at the two people that just walked through the door.

As luck would have it, it was Spinoza and Maria, holding hands and packing heat but also carrying two target posters. The fuckers had printed pictures of me to shoot at just like we did.

"What the hell are you doing here?" I asked Spinoza.

"I'm on a date…what are you doing here?"

"Same thing."

"With a better outcome. You, black girl, you need to pack your bags and leave this town. Girls that date Illy over here usually wind up not waking up the next morning."

"No one tells me what to do, partner. Anyone tries to get at me will get filled with hot lead."

"Suit yourself, I warned you."

Spinoza and Maria took to their shooting booths and hung their posters of me.

"I'll make you a bet, Robin. If we shoot better than you two, then I get to give sexual chocolate over here a peck on the lips."

"What if I win?"

"Then you get to do the same for Maria over here."

"WHAT? NO WAY," Maria spat.

"Deal," I agreed.

"You really gonna let this cracker kiss me?" Sera burned.

"Don't worry, dear. We will win," Spinoza assured my ex-wife.

"Yeah, don't worry, Black dragon. I thrive under pressure." I told Sera.

"If it wasn't just to humiliate Illy, then I'd never let you touch another woman," Maria scowled at Spinoza.

All four of us raised our weapons and got in shooting position. It was a chorus of shots. The rhythm section brought the bangs and Beretta James scat down the lyrics. On their side, things went *HEAD SHOT, HEAD SHOT, HEAD SHOT*. But on our end, it went more *Bang. Ping. Bang. Ping.* Head shots from Sera, misses from me.

The shooting range floor was covered with bullet casings and the room was filled with the peppery smell of gun power. When the smoke cleared, it revealed Spinoza and Maria were the clear winners.

"Woo hoo," Maria jumped with enthusiasm.

I hung my head and watched Spinoza stride over to Sera, who gave him a dead expression of dissatisfaction.

"Fuck you, white boy," she said.

Spinoza just smiled, put his arm around her and kissed her long, hard, and sloppily, dipping her down, swallowing her face into his mouth. When he finally lifted her back up and pulled away, she had to wipe the smeared lipstick off her face.

"Jesus...white boy sure can kiss."

Embarrassed, the only way I could recover any semblance of pride was to hit him where it hurt.

"Hey big shot, how's your case going?"

"It's going fine, now shut your mouth and don't ask me about it again," he spoke, clearly flustered.

"Don't get defensive now, Vic. I know shitty detective work when I see it. Don't worry though, Maria. I've almost got this whole thing wrapped up. I'll know York's killer within the week, I swear to you."

"Really?" Maria suddenly beamed with curiosity, which was her odd way of showing love for me.

"Yep, no thanks to detective dumbass over here."

"That's it, fuck face. You've gone too far."

Spinoza stormed over to me and got an inch away from my face, but I didn't back down.

"What are you gonna do about it?"

"Same thing I used to do to you every day after school. I'm going to give you a wedgie so atomic, you're going to need the jaws of life to pry those tighty whities out of your crack."

"Try me."

"Meet me behind the playground at dusk."

"See you there."

I took Sera by the arm and pulled her out of the range so fast she dropped her gun. Its landing hit the ground so hard that it accidently fired. Vic and Maria ducked and avoided a shot that would've caught them both through the head. Instead, the shot hit the wall and ricocheted right into the poster of my face.

Sera and I returned to my Cadillac and got in.

"Take me home."

"You're supposed to say something to the effect of 'please don't go' or 'you don't need to do this.' You know, talk me out of it."

"Why? I don't give a shit."

"You know...at first I was going to say you reminded me of Mulan."

"The Disney bitch?"

"Yeah, the feminine warrior, able to acquire battle skills rapidly...loyal but now..."

"Bitch, you the princess...I'm the dragon," she shut me down.

I took Sera home and before she left the car, she gave me two simple instructions.

"Kick his ass and never call me."

She slammed the door and I drove off to meet my destiny.

~ * ~

The hallowed halls of Woodrow Wilson high school echoed my name. The phantoms of my thrashings still saturated the air in the stuffy study halls. I recall every drop of blood I left behind. Locker sixty-six and the second toilet on the left in the first boy's room on the right, that's where I'd rest my bones and hang my head.

There was a cool playground breeze brought on by the dusk devils. The American flag waved and buckled at half-mast. Wisps of nostalgia ran their fingers through Vic Spinoza's perfect blonde hair. All the ghosts crowded around the playground, waiting for me to appear. Prepared for battle, I strode onto the war field not wearing any underwear to be wedgied.

"Are you going to put up a fight this one last time?" Vic asked.

"Not on your life. Make this quick, Vic."

"Chicks dig scars and I don't want you out there getting more ass than me."

"You got the one ass that matters."

"She'll love me no matter what happens here."

"Where is she?"

"I told her to stay home."

"I think I'm done talking."

Spinoza balled up his fist and slowly strode toward me. I reverted back to my childhood and squinted with sharp intensity, hoping he would disappear as soon as I reopened my eyes. That's when his fist opened up and planted gently on my shoulder.

"I'm not going to fight you, Illy," he said softly as I opened my eyes.

"What are you going to do?"

"Ask for your help...I'm at a dead end in this case..."

"I don't work with the city."

"I had a few men tail Sera...do you think that'll make a difference?"

"No."

"Neither do I. They go out with you and they die...so why do you keep dating?"

"I guess I'm the epitome of a hopeless romantic."

"Listen, I got a few tests back from the lab, new info."

"Care to share?"

"If you do the same."

"You first."

I pulled out a cigarette and lit it, my foot tapping as I waited for him to cave in and give me the goods.

"The guy's index finger prints had a strange insignia in the swirl. From what I could tell, it looks like a small winking Hitler."

"Winking Hitler?"

"It could be Chaplin but it's probably Hitler...Hitler if the perp is rich, Chaplin if he's poor, I figure."

"He's rich, alright. A poor killer would've felt those girls up if he ever got the chance to be that close to them."

"You might be right...we also discovered fibers of the same steel blade."

"Japanese katana."

Spinoza's bushy blonde eyebrows rose, furled and danced with curiosity until clenching with his whole face, angrily realizing I was most likely ahead of him in solving the case.

"Why do you say that?"

"Go big or go home...that's this psycho's modus operandi."

"Sounds like you're hot on his trail."

"Burning up."

"I don't suppose you'd share the glory."

"The glory would never accept you."

"How'd you get so good at this gig anyway, Robin?"

"If I didn't get good at finding killers, I might've ended up becoming one...all thanks to you, Vic."

"Should I say you're welcome?"

"No...just treat her good...she's one of a kind."

"I will."

I let the wind fill in the blanks between us then took off, simply vanishing into the fog.

~ * ~

After two days of rest, relaxation, and tabulation, I got a call from the still breathing Sera.

"I thought you never wanted to talk to me again?" I said as soon as I answered the phone.

"I told *you* not to call *me*, now I'm calling you. You need to learn to listen."

"You're right, what's up?"

"I'm on lockdown in my own apartment. Three cops are here, watching every move I make and not letting me go outside, all because of you."

"Blame Randolph, he should've told you there was a catch."

"Randolph is why I'm calling you. He wants you to meet him at his office today at four p.m."

"Why couldn't he just tell me himself?"

"I don't know, you ought to ask him."

"Tell him I'll be there...any chance I can swing by with some dinner tonight seeing as you can't go out?"

"I'd rather starve...besides these cops are protecting me from you, Illy."

She hung up the phone and I shrugged off my regrets. At four p.m. I headed over to Royce Tower downtown.

Part II:

The Chase is Better Than the Catch

Chapter Thirteen

The Formula

The steel colossus shimmered in the pale sunlight. Majesty carved from a raw obelisk of gold, the building stood fifty stories high. I parked and strutted up a flight of stairs that led to a black marble fountain where Rodan's Thinker shot water out of his head. I flicked in a penny and made a wish for world bliss then hustled into the tower.

Security patted me down and felt up Beretta James underneath my pant leg then asked me to hand her over.

"I'm Royce's personal P.I. He wants me packing at all times."

"Really? You wouldn't mind if I called him to confirm that, would you? If your story checks out, hell, I'll give you a few bullets."

The security guard opened up a drawer to show me all the confiscated guns, bullets, blades, and fireworks. He then slammed it shut and called Royce directly. They shared a brief but telling bullet-point dialogue.

"Yeah...Robin...got a gun...nope...okay..." he put the phone down and turned to me with a pugnacious scowl. "I'm sorry, Mr. Robin, but the gun stays. You can have it back on your way out."

"Take care of that piece. I put a curse on it that effects everyone that handles it."

"Including you?"

"Sometimes sacrifices have to be made. Did Mr. Royce sound scared of me?"

"People don't get to the fiftieth floor of their own tower being scared of guys like you."

I was waved over by an escort and followed him to the elevator, an obnoxiously elegant chamber. I stepped in, had the escort swipe his key card for verification then I pushed the button above forty-nine which read "RR." A swift bounce down then I was shot up the golden palace. The elevator was designed to play a brief video history of Randolph Royce's life with images that enveloped you from every side. Each floor represented that year of his life, so floor one began with his birth. His mother seemed rather uncaring for the life that just popped out of her. Not once did she look him in the eyes.

I ascended from birth to baby carriage to college graduation to his wedding to today, here and now. Randolph Royce, the man of fifty years and stories. What's he going to do next year? Build another floor? I got off on the RR penthouse and immediately stepped into a soft twenty-four karat golden hallway. Every step left an imprint in the malleable floor that gave me the sinking feeling of drowning in wealth. Dante appeared in front of me and nodded.

"Follow me, Mr. Robin, and don't do anything suspicious."

"Fine, one question though...do you remember Monty Freed?"

"No, but I find asking me that rather questionable."

I shut up and Dante led me past a gallery of oil portraits of Randolph with his German shepherds. Each one was signed in the corner by A.W. My favorite was of Randolph in a white, eighties Miami Vice style jacket, on the beach surrounded by native women from the pacific islands. When we reached Royce's office, Dante turned to me and firmly pressed his hand on my scalp.

"When you go in there, don't touch anything you're not supposed to. Don't go looking around and don't let your curiosity get you killed, understand?"

I was so frightened and paralyzed by his grip, all I could do was blink twice for "okay."

"Good boy," he pinched my cheek and led me into the office.

The double doors were large and gold with ivory handles that curled like tusks. Dante opened the door and instructed me, "Take a seat, Mr. Royce will be here shortly."

The view from his office was so awesome it magnetized me right past his luxury furniture. I could see all of Los Angeles, from the Hollywood Hills to the Pacific and on every street the poor and homeless mingled and bumped into each other like ants without a queen.

"You can understand how staring out that window makes it hard to sympathize with them, can't you?"

I turned and Randolph was behind me holding a bouquet of flowers.

"Aww, you shouldn't have."

"Shut up, they're for a date tonight," Royce fumed.

"Why wouldn't you let me bring my gun, Royce? You have nothing to be afraid of."

"I don't? All these girls I connected you with are dead."

"Except Sera."

"Really? Have you checked the news today?"

Randolph walked over to his desk and opened a drawer to take out a remote control. He pressed a button and the entire right side of his office slid up and revealed a giant screen, already on the news.

A reporter was speaking over video, outside of Sera's apartment in Inglewood where police taped off the entrance.

"Sera Dippity, a resident of Inglewood, has been shot along with two policemen, Officers Carey Grass and Pete Morton, in a standoff with Officer Mike Shep. All three police officers, including Shep, were on patrol, protecting Sera. Sometime today, Officer Shep appeared to have snapped, in what is being called a spontaneous psychotic episode then shot at and took the lives of both his partners and Sera before taking his own."

"Now what would compel a cop to do that?" I asked.

"What would a guy need a gun in my office for?"

"Why be suspicious if you know I have an alibi?"

"What do all these girls have in common?"

"They dated you, Randolph."

"They also dated you, Illy."

"They all rejected me."

"I rejected them, so who's got more motive?"

"Still doesn't take the cop into account."

"That's why I think you're clean but can't be sure."

Randolph put the television on mute and sat down behind his desk with a long, deflating sigh. I had done him in.

"Why'd you go through Sera to get me here?" I asked.

"We can't be associated anymore. That means no more employment or contact. My matchmaking days for you are over."

"If you're not my employer anymore, then you wouldn't mind answering some questions about your relationship with David York."

"The attorney? He handled my divorce, the fat bastard."

"You know he's dead too, right? The police think it's the same guy that's behind our girls."

He swiveled his chair until it pointed sharply at me. I read his glare and knew he thought I suspected him.

"Who do you think did it?" he asked me.

"It's who the killer's working for that I care about."

"I wouldn't put it past my ex-wife, in that case."

"Having been divorced, I know where you're coming from, but you and York's relationship went beyond his representation, am I right? You crossed well into the realm of criminality with him."

"Oh, you know about that?"

"I didn't take you for a drug kingpin, Royce."

"I used to have a little bowling club called the Sixth Pin back in the day. Sixth as in 666, the number of the beast and pin as in king pin, as in me. I don't play that game anymore though because the common drug user reached such a low point, drugs actually did them more good than harm."

"You sound like a super villain."

"Villainy is the key to success in this country. Look through my window at all of those tiny vermin down there thinking they're heroes. Heroism is what keeps them down there."

"You're not a murderer...because killing is hard work. As much blood as you spill, it requires equal sweat and you sir, have never worked up an honest sweat in your goddamn life."

"How dare you? You creepy little goof. After all I've done for you, I paid you well, I gave you my women, now you stand in my office trying to discredit my ethic? Where is your honor?? Where is your loyalty?" Randolph growled through teeth that automatically clenched up whenever he got offended.

"My only loyalty is to my honor. Every L.A. dick codifies a set of unwritten rules, only I wrote them down. At the top of that list is something I like it to call 'calling it how I see it,' so I see you and I call you a sad little rich kid getting revenge on the world for letting him have everything but love...because love is earned, friend. That's what all this villainy is about, not letting anyone else be happy either."

"Where's your love, Illy?"

"Not in my way of seeing clearly, I know that."

"It's not anywhere at all...and definitely not in my hands anymore."

"I'm not afraid to die alone, Randolph. I'm afraid to live in a world where guys like you get to make decisions."

"You should be. Now get the hell out of my office."

There was nothing left to say. The air was so thick with his sense of revulsion toward me, I started choking up a bit. I walked to the door and heard him spit. Dante was waiting for me outside the office with a packed fist that he sent right into my stomach, crumpling up my guts.

"Ungrateful types like you make me sick."

I was barely able to stand until he grabbed me by the back of my jacket and dragged me to the elevator then threw me in and pressed the button for the bottom floor. I was sitting down, holding my aching stomach as the elevator descended and I watched Royce's life pass by in reverse. He was infantilized before my very eyes. I had to wonder where it all went wrong. At floor twenty-nine, I saw the scene of his wedding. Doves carried white roses over the heads of hundreds of happy faces, gathered to see Royce commit to share his life with someone. The elevator stopped and before the doors slid open, I stood up to avoid any unwanted questions. A beautiful woman carrying a bag of Chinese takeaway boxes stumbled in to join me.

"Geez, what is with these elevators? The last one just plain old stopped two floors below and I had to take the stairs carrying this heavy load."

"This machine is all flash and no guts, these days people would rather make things look nice than work properly."

"What's so nice looking about this?"

She scanned the scene, unimpressed by all the money he must've put into his elevator and wedding.

I shrugged, "It looks like it was a pretty extravagant occasion wouldn't you say?"

"Yeah but where's the love?" she kept looking around the room, finding nothing until fixing her stare back at me. I'm not sure why but we looked into each other's eyes for almost half a minute until I felt myself on the verge of tears. I had to smile just to draw them back.

"Sorry, what floor did you need?" I nervously asked to break the tender awkwardness.

"Fifty."

"Oh," she was Royce's date. I sighed and hung my head, unable to hide my disappointment.

"What?" she asked.

"Nothing...it's just..."

"What?"

"This elevator's going down," I looked up at her.

Her eyes snapped open as she realized she'd have to wait to go the whole way down just to start all over again. Her reflexes sprang up as she tried to make a mad dash out but the doors slid closed, beginning our descent.

"Shit."

"Don't worry, girls as beautiful as you don't need to rush."

She blushed then hissed out a laugh, "*tsssssss*".

"What's your name?" I asked.

"Jessica Steinman, what's yours?"

"Illy Robin, it's nice to..."

The elevator shook from side to side and came to a dead halt after passing floor twenty-one. We stopped at the scene of Randolph getting legally drunk for the first time until it faded away with the overhead lights, leaving us in complete darkness.

"Oh, my god...what just happened?" Jessica panicked.

I frantically pressed every button and turned every knob but it was no use. With all my strength, I could only pull the doors open a crack to see the innards of Royce tower between floors twenty-one and twenty. My arms gave out and the doors snapped shut like the mouth of a crocodile, leaving us there to rot.

"We're stuck...."

"Damn it, you gotta be kidding me." She planted her bag of Chinese food and ass down on the floor.

I sat down and tried to make her face out in the darkness. I saw her clear as day only moments ago, but now I was dying to remember every contour. She pulled her phone out and its brightness illuminated her face. Hers was a face that lit up the room and my heart, melting away my sorrow. She dialed a number and brought the phone to her ear.

"Hello Randolph...? Yeah, it's Jessica... No, I'm stuck in the elevator...between floors twenty and twenty-one... I don't know why, it's not my fault...who cares what I think of the elevator, can you get me out of here...? How long will that take...? No, I'm here all alone..." I wonder why she lied, "Fine, just be quick, thanks..."

"Why didn't you tell him I was here?"

"Because guys like him get jealous if their date smiles in the same picture as another man."

She had a good read on him.

"What's in the bag?"

"Shrimp fried rice, kung pao chicken, orange chicken, beef and broccoli, and a bottle of my favorite Moscato."

"Open the Moscato."

"I was saving it for my date."

"You don't think Randolph has his own?"

"I'm sure he does, but I thought it would be a nice gesture."

"Sharing a drink in this situation would be much more generous."

"I guess it would, yeah."

She pulled the wine and opener out of her bag and passed them to me.

"You open it."

If I soiled the cork, I knew I'd taint the moment and its memory for the rest of my days, so I gripped the bottle and punctured the cork with focused pressure then wound down the opener, penetrating deep into the pink. I pulled up the cork, popped the bottle open then passed it back to Jessica.

"Take the first whiff."

She took the bottle and brought her nose to its lip and I could see the smell transport her far away from this place. She then took a long sip of three gulps and passed it back to me.

"Mmmmm... So good."

I took the bottle and indulged myself, tasting her lips as I drank.

"It's delicious, where'd you buy it?"

"My neighborhood Booze Hound...he's the best one I know, he can get you the stuff you can't find anywhere."

"Awesome...you're not homeless, though, are you?"

"No, but most of my friends are... I swear, artists ought to have their own economic class someday...these friends keep telling me to abandon the house life but I can't, my grandparents built that house."

"No shame in gentle living. I'm just like you but I got an apartment."

She took another sip from the bottle. Already the buzz began to daze.

"When I was in high school, three friends and I finished a keg in one night."

"Holy shit, that's over fifty beers."

"We all blacked out and puked."

"Pass the bottle...I need to get on your level."

Once it went from her hands to mine then to my lips, I was off, chugging.

"Hey, don't Bogart our only liquid."

Once I released the bottle from my mouth, I belched and passed it back. She laughed so hard she snorted.

"What's a goof like you doing with an ass like Randolph?"

"I'm a private investigator."

Her disbelief prevented her from laughing.

"That's so cool."

"Thanks."

"Is Randolph being investigated or did he hire you?"

"Both...any more than that you don't want to know."

"Sure I do, I'm about to go on a date with this guy."

"You really want to know?"

"Yes...not to mention, as a painter, my talent is to see the big picture and apply it on canvas piece by piece. When a piece is missing, it doesn't take me long to figure out what belongs there. If you give me the picture of your case, I'll fill in the blanks."

"I don't know what it is with me and painters. The last one said I was her muse and turned out to be a suspect in this murder case."

"Anyone musing about you has got to have a few screws loose."

I laughed, "Okay fine...this case begins with my ex-wife Maria, asking me to solve her second husband's murder. This guy, David York's his name, was my divorce attorney..."

"Wow, what an asshole."

"Exactly, everyone and their mother had a motive. Anyway, his body was found on the streets, neck slit open with a Pacifica cigar sticking out the hole."

"Geez..."

"Meanwhile, I was tracking down Randolph's daughter for him."

"Oh, you know Dorothy? That's how I met Randolph. Dorothy and I went to art school together. She was one of the girls that finished the keg with me."

"She's a good girl, don't know where she gets that good from though."

"Her mom is the best, nothing like Randolph."

"That's good to hear...anyway, so as a reward for bringing Dorothy back, Randolph becomes my matchmaker and sets up all these dates for me with girls he's been out with before. One by one, after every date, the girl gets killed."

"What the fuck...how?"

"Usually with blades; the first to her back, the second got mauled by dogs then cut to pieces. The third and fourth got carved up. The most recent one that died today, she was under police supervision. Lo and behold, one of the officers went ballistic, killing her and the two other cops."

"I saw that on TV today."

"Now you know what's really going on."

"This is so interesting..." she took a long gulp of the wine, polishing it off to the last drop. "Give me a minute...I'm thinking...your clues are the cigar, the dogs, and a blade, right?"

"Oh, I forgot to mention, I'm being followed by this kid recording every move I make on camera and his henchman, who took two of the women home after our dates. This henchman owned David York's favorite bar, knew his favorite song, and also tipped me off to one of Randolph Royce's old businesses, The Sixth Pin which had 'Eat the Rich' spray painted on the back wall."

"Eat the Rich?"

"Sorry, there's still more I left out... So 'Eat the Rich' is the signature of this one unknown graffiti artist named Rawr, who I think is Rocky Rude. She's the psycho who calls me her muse. I met Rocky on a date planned by Randolph then took another date to her art show. Every victim I just described was painted in a perfect depiction of their murder. That night I was knocked out by someone wearing a black glove so I couldn't stop her from being killed."

"Rocky Rude? I know that name."

"Is she big in the art world?"

"She's not small... Oh, I remember now, Rocky Rude's not her real name...she's Allison Watson; she paints Royce's portraits."

"The one's with the dogs and girls?"

"Yeah, I'm not a big fan but she knows how to reproduce a face onto canvas."

"I guess I'll be checking her out next."

"If we ever get out of this elevator."

"I'm not sure I want to anymore," I smiled and affectionately gazed at Jessica.

Jessica smirked, "You hungry? Want some Chinese?"

"Sure."

She pulled out a box of chicken chow mein and two sets of chop sticks. We both picked at the noodles, and slurped them in, getting our faces greasy in the darkness.

"The only reason I accepted this date is because I was curious how someone as rich as Randolph treats a girl, but now I think I'm going to go snooping around and do my own detective work for you."

"I wouldn't. If Randolph catches on, he'll have both of our heads on sticks."

"I can't stop thinking about this case now."

Suddenly, a bright light shined through the pried open elevator doors. Elevator maintenance and security finally came to our rescue. As our pupils readjusted to the light and their blurry faces sharpened up, Jessica realized Royce wasn't even there to meet her.

"Where's Randolph?"

"On call in his office. Come with me, I'll take you to him."

"Mr. Robin, what are you doing here? Ms. Steinman said she was all alone," the security guard asked.

"I tried to rescue her and got trapped inside."

"How on earth did you do that?"

"Use your imagination."

"I'll use the security footage, thanks."

"Fair enough...just let me have my gun and I'll be out of your hair."

I reached into my jacket, sneakily pulled out my business card, and slipped it into Jessica's bag. Maintenance pulled us out of the elevator and forced us to split. Now in the light, I could see how terribly the chow mein had oiled up our faces.

"You got a little schmutz." I circled my finger around my face.

"So do you," she said and we both grinned.

I never had a greater inkling to kiss someone, it felt like a sin to let her go. The look in my eyes communicated to her the most elegant farewell and I could tell by the look in her eyes that she translated it perfectly.

"Goodbye, Jessica."

"Bye, Illy."

I tried to wink but couldn't isolate my nerve endings to just one eye so I blinked. She giggled and I walked away blushing. I left Royce tower with a new spring in my step. A lover's swagger. A romantic's romp. I mean, here was a girl I could see myself protecting from the stain Adolf Hitler left on the world. I got in my car and was compelled to drive fast until I felt invincible. Sloppy at times, my mind drifted off the road to tiny flashes of her tiny features. Her nose's curl, her hair's fine chop, that soda pop bottle shape. I had to tell someone but without a rooftop to shout from,

I settled for Carino. I found him outside of my office, smoking a joint on the stoop.

"You won't ever guess what happened to me."

"You met a beautiful girl and you're in love...what has it been, only ten minutes since you first laid eyes upon her?"

"More like thirty but how'd you know?"

"You're standing up straight, your foot lost its hobble, your face lifted a few millimeters up from its usual droop, your eyes look clear, your hair's messy, and your hands are shaking...you seem schizophrenically happy but just don't get obsessed, you have a murder to solve."

"This is my only chance. I don't care if it makes me drop this case. I don't care if it kills me."

"Do you care if it kills her?"

I clenched my fist then jumped on Carino. He triggered something in me. Happy and ready to fight, without ever needing or desiring a warning, Carino scrapped with me right there on the street. We threw short punches to each other's faces and bodies, scratching ourselves against the concrete's unforgiving grain. I pushed him off of me and sat down on the stoop beside him then as coolly as a breeze changes directions, we arrived back at peace.

"You're right, she might already be a target," I commiserated.

"I doubt it."

"Why?"

"Because the one's you don't love are the ones that die."

"What are you saying?"

"If you fall in love with this girl, then that breaks the pattern and this killer can't work outside a pattern."

"In other words, she'll break the curse."

"In some Peter-Pan-lost-boy-never-wanna-grow-up kind of way, yeah. If you date her and she doesn't fall in love with you, she's as dead as a doorknob."

"What should I do?"

"You have to find the killer before you date the girl."

"What if that takes so long it kills my momentum?"

"Then I suggest you hurry up."

My only untapped lead was Rocky Rude. No doubt she was still angry at me for bringing Lucy to her art show, but perhaps Lucy's death made her feel better. I would have to go in with the confidence that as her muse, I could play her heart strings like a fiddle.

Basking in the sunset behind my windshield, I came up on Rocky Rude's beachside studio where I saw a sign, 'Beware all ye who create.' Bewaring but uncaring, I lit a cigarette and entered through her unlocked front door. As soon as I stepped inside, I saw her naked back turned to me as her ass perched on a stool, revealing her crack and a tattoo of a panther running down her back. She was swabbing carnelian red into a painting of Lucy's body, making the wound. Lucy was unraveled out of her Persian rug with her back all carved and stabbed up. Those hands covered in dry paint that crusted into every fingernail's crevice couldn't commit such a gruesome murder just like Lucy suggested. No paint particles were discovered at the scene. Furthermore, if she was painting Lucy unwrapped out of the rug, she must be painting a moment after the body had been discovered by police. Lo and Behold, perched up at the side of the canvas by a safety pin, was an LAPD crime scene photograph of Lucy.

I floated up to Rocky and rested my hand on her neck, massaging it ever so soothingly. Her hand stopped moving as if frozen by my icy chill, and I saw her take her anger out on the painting, pushing the brush against the painting until crushing the bristles, deepening the red wound she was dabbing.

"I hate you so much," the brush fell out of her grip and she covered her face with her hands, probably getting paint in her eyes as she wept.

"Why?"

"For not being who I need you to be," she spoke between snivels.

"Who?"

"I need you to be an adult, but you're acting like a child."

"How?"

"A child doesn't appreciate anything. They go through one toy to the next, without a care. Can't you recognize the best thing for you when it comes around? You and I, we're what's best for each other," she broke down harder, tears rolling down her breasts as they hung off her collapsing chest.

"You never told me you felt this way, Rocky."

"You're supposed to read me and know I was lying because I don't think I deserve love sometimes...I had a hard life, Illy, just like you."

"Rocky, are you hurting these girls that you're painting?"

"No, I get these pictures from the LAPD...I don't like painting such violent things. If I could, I'd only paint love...but I have to pay the bills. It just so happens my patrons want violence."

"Who wants it, Rocky?"

"I can't say...they paid for my silence."

"Is it Randolph Royce? I know you paint all of his portraits."

"Don't interrogate me, Illy. Don't hurt the only person that loves you."

"You don't know me."

"So? Like you've never fallen in love this fast?"

She put her hands down, looked up at me as if she knew I fell in love as hard and quickly as she did all of the time, every time.

"You're right, I do...but I didn't with you."

"Just take me out, please...you'll see, you'll love me."

I paused. My pity for her took over. She reminded me of myself. I had been rejected so many times, why should I think I'm too good for her? Why should I not give her the chance?

"If I don't feel the same way as you do by the end of it, will you be hurt?"

"Yes."

I felt her pain, I swear I did.

"You know what happens to girls that go out with me, right?"

"I don't care...this is our only chance."

"I'll pick you up tomorrow night at eight."

Tomorrow was the third of July. Midnight would ring in the most romantic twenty-four hours of the year. The explosive release of a year's worth of suppressed American dreaming.

"Can we watch the fireworks together?" Her tears retreated as my affirmation beckoned.

"Yes."

She jumped off of her stool, embraced me, wrapping her arms

around my neck, kissing my face all over. Even her tears took on the sweet taste of joy.

"Thank you, thank you, thank you so much, sweetheart."

With my chin perched on her shoulder, I felt a vibration in my pants. I received a text. I took my phone out of my pocket to look at it behind Rocky's back. It was Jessica.

Hey Illy, it's Jessica. I found your card in my bag. It was so nice meeting you. Listen, I did some snooping on my 'date' and look what I found.

A picture appeared of Jessica smoking a Pacifica cigar on a bed, hers I prayed.

Don't I look badass?

Playing off my shock, I put my phone away and kissed Rocky goodbye on the cheek. I walked out of the studio, hobbling again. All the gusto Jessica injected me with had been harvested. As I approached my car and put my hand on the door handle, I looked out to the ocean at high tide. I thought of all the movies and books I've ever read where someone just strolls right into the Pacific with all their clothes on to drown. What a terrible way to go I thought...only in L.A.

Chapter Fourteen

A Tale of Tails

Standing there, in the buff, fresh out of dreamland, I took a good look at myself in the mirror, and in myself I could see all the women I dated. Everyone I ever knew, everyone I ever touched, had slept inside me that night. Even with such brief contact, something from each date rubbed off and summed up to what some would call confidence. I treated ever girl fairly well with the exception of the only one who actually wanted me, Rocky Rude. No matter how confident I felt, spreading the skin of my face, I could not mistake that one crack for what it was, guilt. Even if I didn't see a future with her, I wanted to reciprocate her feelings for just one night, if for no other reason than to make up for the coldness the world showed me.

I took my best jacket, slacks, and shirt to the dry cleaners and got a haircut. I spent the day in the bookstore memorizing romantic poetry. Then when my dry cleaning was ready and I had to pick my clothes up, I received a text from Jessica.

Did you speak to Rocky Rude?

Yes.

Meet me tonight at the Santa Monica Roller Dome and tell me about it.

I can't, I made plans with her.

That's even better, bring her too, she responded.

I approached the drycleaners in my car as I coasted up the street, phone in hand. Glancing down from the road to Jessica's text, I accidently drove past the dry cleaners and decided this was some kind of omen to leave my clothes there and dress casually for the Roller Dome. I glanced back down at the text and started typing.

What time?

Nine p.m.

My heart sank from my chest to stomach and was feasted upon by the butterflies. I drove home to dress down. I threw on my denim jacket and jeans, a horizontally striped black and white T-shirt, a paper boy cap, and blue suede shoes. I drove out to the beach and parked my car in Rocky's driveway then left it in park, running. I came out of the car, honked the horn, and leaned against the hood waiting for her, smoking an oceanic cigarette through a soft crackle. I closed my eyes until I heard Rocky's door open and close. When I opened my eyes, I saw she was wearing a beautiful, black dress and heels and black pearl necklace. She got her hair done and nails polished. Every speck of paint and dirt was washed off of her skin. She had been transformed into her best self, which was a different person.

"You look beautiful."

Feeling treasured, her batting eyelashes dotted and dashed up and down, telling me "thank you" in Morse-code. She stared at my blue suede shoes then panned up to my paperboy cap, taking me in.

"Are we going to a rock show in 1974?"

"It's a surprise."

"I'm starving."

"Let's go, I don't want us to be late."

She walked over to the passenger's side of my car and stood there as I got behind the wheel, put the car in reverse, and was ready to go.

"What's wrong?" I lurched my head at her, puzzled.

"I went through a lot of trouble to look and feel this good for you, so I'll be damned if you don't open the door for me."

"Sorry," I opened my door and stepped off the brake to get out, totally forgetting that I left the car in reverse. The car started backing out of the driveway.

"Shit," I scrambled.

Rocky put her hand over her brow and just shook her head. I ran after the car, dove into driver's seat, stomped on the brake and put the car in drive then parked it right back up to Rocky Rude. I got out, again, swept over to Rocky's side and held her door open for her.

"Thank you, dear," she kissed me on the cheek, unsusceptible to my sabotage.

She got in the car and I swung back behind the wheel and drove us out of her driveway and through Santa Monica. We drove in silence at first, so I decided to break the waves by turning right on the radio dial. Rocky's hand rested upon mine and she guided the dial back left to silence.

"What are you thinking about?" She gazed at me with prying eyes.

"My case."

"Even with a beautiful woman sitting right next to you?"

I turned to her, wanting my words to nurture her.

"If it weren't for the beautiful woman sitting right next to me, then this case would've overwhelmed me to the point of giving up and that's if I was lucky."

She leaned in and put her head onto my shoulder. I tilted my rearview mirror down to see what kind of couple we were. We were separate beings on separate journeys pulled together by forced intimacy. I only had one foot in her moment. I didn't feel nervous, I felt like an asshole, like I could get away with treating her terribly. I silently thanked every woman who ever rejected me for not being as selfish as I felt now.

"We're here."

She floated off of my shoulder and opened her eyes to see me drive into the Santa Monica Roller Dome.

"The Roller Dome?"

"It's going to be a great game."

Her stomach growled and her eyes puppied up.

"I'll buy us some nachos and cola, don't worry," I assured her.

I parked and turned off my car, opened my door, swung around, and opened hers. I took her out and when she stood up, I raised my arm for her to waltz under it.

"I wish you took me to dinner and dancing."

"Maybe some other time."

I shut the door and we drifted together but apart to the dome. The Roller Dome's interior was a zoo with children crying and screaming, fat men and women leaving trails of trash, and the reek of sweat in the air. God bless the U. S. of A.

Rocky was so well dressed that she attracted every man's gaze, whistles, and cat calls wherever she went.

"Hey baby, get that sweet ass over here."

She fled to me and clung to my arm, her nails digging into the denim.

"I want to leave."

"We just got here, the game hasn't even started."

"Good, these people are animals."

I stopped, turned to her, and put my hands on her shoulders looking her dead in the eye. I took my cap off to seem more like myself and our minds connected.

"Rocky, I know this wasn't what you were expecting, but this is where I want us to be... trust me, Rocky. Trust that I know how to tend to your heart, okay?"

"Okay," she spoke softly and nodded slowly.

I led her by the arm to the concessions stand and bought us a jumbo tub of popcorn, some nachos with loads of sharp melted cheddar, and two medium RC colas. We found a pair of seats in the front row of the rink and sat down.

"Rocky, I got a question."

"Yes, dear?"

"You said you started with your career doing graffiti, so I was wondering if you've ever heard of a street artist named Rawr?"

"Sure, I'm a fan."

"Have you ever seen them in person?"

"I bet I have, only I didn't realize it was them at the time. I've followed his career for a while and even read a few books about him. "

"Really? Do you what the significance of his pseudonym 'Rawr' is?"

"He's a cat person, a jungle cat person. "

"Oh, I just assumed they were their initials...Rocky Allison Watson Rude..."

She glared at me in disbelief. "How did you..."

A siren sounded off and both teams rushed out from their tunnels into the roller rink. It was the Murder City Maidens against Team

Horsepower. Dressed in red and black just like the rest of the Maidens, Jessica came out swinging hips and punches. A male referee rolled up to the center of the rink and the sirens stopped.

"Ladies and gentlemen, children of all ages, Santa Monica Roller Dome would like to welcome you to another night of debauchery and damage as the Murder City Maidens take on Team Horsepower."

The audience clapped, cheered and threw popcorn at the ref.

"Before the games begin, I would just like to remind you of the rules in this evening's match. These brave women will be participating in a Last Woman Standing match where a team becomes victorious when every member of the opposite team is eliminated by fall. If a girl is able to get the ball into the net for a goal, then one eliminated teammate is allowed back into the match," the referee finished.

"Is this going to be violent? I hate violence," Rocky asked me.

Jessica rolled up to our seats and leaned against the fiber glass wall separating us.

"Mr. Robin, glad you could make it."

"No problem, just don't hurt yourself."

"With you watching? Never."

She smiled then rolled back to her teammates.

"Who was that?"

"A business associate, friends don't address me as Mr. Robin."

"I hope she gets her ugly fat head chopped off," Rocky fumed.

The referee threw the ball up into the air, beginning the match. The roller girls circled the rink at diabolical speeds. The ball dropped back into the rink and bounced right into the arms of Team Horsepower's captain. To a hail of cheers and applause, the captain raised her free fist while holding the ball close. Apparently not close enough though because Jessica was hauling ass behind her, until goring her straight into the fiber glass barrier. The captain lost the ball and her teeth and Jessica was there for the rebound.

"What a cow," Rocky snarled.

Jessica carried the ball with two Team Horsepower girls hot on her tail. Seeing them out the corner of her eye, Jessica spun around and elbowed both girls in the face, breaking their noses and making them tumble out. Jessica came in close proximity to the net, thrust the ball in and scored.

"Why did we come somewhere to watch ugly girls, wearing ugly clothes, doing ugly things?" Rocky asked and rolled her eyes.

"Because it's beautiful," I replied.

The game continued with Team Horsepower's ball. Like a runaway train, Jessica pistoned past her team and careened into the enemy, toppling four girls and knocking them unconscious. The blood-stained rink became her yard. She snarled like a pit-bull-pit-boss as the remaining girls were too scared to make a break for the ball until it was too late and Jessica made a break for them. Now every member of Team Horsepower had been eliminated. The referee returned to the rink and blew his whistle.

"Sudden death, rumble rules, every girl for herself," the ref announced.

Jessica set her sights onto her own team and one after another, she savagely ravaged through every girl in her way. Once the dust settled and the cheers were hushed by the polarizing picture of ten broken women in her wake, Jessica was still standing with her hand raised.

"Are you entertained?" Jessica asked the audience, who responded with a hail of trash and cheer.

"No," Rocky shouted at her.

Jessica spat out her mouth-guard.

"I challenge any of you. Man or Woman. If you think you're tough, step into my world."

Everyone started looking around waiting for someone to accept her challenge until Rocky stood up out of her seat and every pair of eyes fell on her.

"Are you crazy, she'll eat you alive," I pled while tugging at Rocky's dress, trying to get her to sit back down.

Rocky stood there for a moment and I noticed she was crying, almost whimpering. The referee opened the rink's corral door for her to enter, but instead of hopping through, the tears started streaming and she ran out of our row, up the aisle, then out of the Roller Dome completely.

"Rocky. Wait," I shot up out of my seat and followed her.

I burst through the entrance doors and saw her crying in the parking lot, spinning in circles as if trying to find an escape from her emotional prison.

"*No more love, no more sweethearts, no more happy endings,*" Rocky muttered to herself manically.

"Rocky, please stop crying, I'm sorry," I shouted as I approached.

She stopped spinning and fixed her eyes on me, in total meltdown mode.

"I just wanted to sit across from you somewhere nice and quiet so we could talk and get to know each other and try to love each other but what did you do? You threw me away like garbage. And for what!? For her!?"

She started clubbing my chest with her fists until I grabbed both her wrists and restrained her.

"If I don't love you, don't love me."

"I can't, I have to," she sounded ravaged.

"Have to? Nobody has to?"

"Yes, I do," her tears twisted her voice to a shriek.

"I will never love you, Rocky," and with that, her arms went limp in my grasp and she stopped fighting.

"Stop..." she begged.

"There's nothing you can do..."

"Please...stop."

"I never want to see you again," I finished, coldly.

She wailed like a dying animal and pulled her wrists out of my hands then ran off into the night. Heavy hearted, I just watched her go until Jessica came up from behind me and lightened things up.

"You were right about her, what a nut-bar."

I couldn't help but laugh even though I wanted to cry.

"I feel terrible," I said, shaking my head.

"You should."

"I'm such an ass-hat."

"You are."

"I'm never going to lead a girl on ever again," I promised.

"You won't," she assured me.

I stopped laughing and we glanced at each other for a moment and settled into each other's company.

"It's still early, do you want to get some drinks?" I asked her.

"Oh, absolutely. I know a house party."

"Screw the party. I know a bar."

She took me by the arm and I led her back to my parked car. We both got in and I drove to the nearest beachside dive. The bar contained a wild crowd, all pounding down pints and shots and cocktails and wine. The salty sea spray wafted into the room and comingled with the cigar smoke, giving the bar the aroma of smoked cod. The jukebox rocked with a roaring saxophone reaming everyone up the taint as they danced and caroused around it. I led Jessica through the line of people waiting to order their drinks and out of drunken courtesy for a cripple, the drunks let me go ahead of them.

"What do you want?" asked the bartender.

I turned to Jessica.

"Something tropical," she said.

"Two vodka pineapples," I ordered, giving them a peace sign.

This was the first time I ordered anything that wasn't a Jameson on the rocks in over a decade. She was already expanding my horizons and forcing me out of my comfort zone.

Our mellow yellow drinks were sloshed out onto the bar and we clinked them together and cheered *"Na sdarovye."*

We guzzled our drinks and slammed our finished glasses back down on the bar then she pulled me over to the dance floor. We hopped, jived and swiveled at each other until a drunk lit off a firework indoors that whizzed across the room, exploding into the wall of booze behind the bar. The eruption sent the fire alarm ringing and sprinklers dousing us down. We scampered out of the bar with the rest of the patrons, still thirsty. We found the beach boardwalk's Booze Hound and bought an old, bootlegged-booby-trapped-cobweb bottle of Raider's Rum to drink in my car.

She popped open the bottle, took a swig, and passed it to me. I took a swig, wiped my lips and stared straight through the windshield into the foggy void.

"That Pacifica cigar you found."

"Yeah, Royce's."

"That's hard evidence, you know...that might get us somewhere."

"Wait till I get in his house, I'll find you something really scandalous."

"Have you ever been to his house? He's got eyes on everything."

"He invited me over tomorrow night."

I turned quiet, trying not to appear jealous and give away that I was falling for her madly.

"I didn't do anything with him, Illy."

I stared right at her, giving myself away.

"I never would," she continued.

"I don't want money. I don't want him."

"What do you want?" I asked.

"Justice for these girls...and to solve this damned case."

"I'm solving this case, babe. Don't forget it."

She smirked, "Not if I do first...you going to drink that?" She looked down at the bottle of rum and I returned it to her.

She took another sip.

"You know where Rocky lives?" she continued.

"Yeah."

"Let's go there."

"Why?"

"My detective senses are tingling," Jessica joked.

"Hasn't she suffered enough?"

"Just enough to be vulnerable and do something drastic."

"A stake out is no slumber party, Jessica."

"I could stay up all night, I'm so revved up."

"Fine, we'll grab some drive-thru and watch her for an hour."

"Can we go to the house party? I promise you won't want to miss it."

"No, this is the party," I said while putting the car in gear and driving off.

By the time we arrived at the drive-thru's pick-up window, Jessica was half outside the car, half in, puking out all of the booze she had just ingested. This sight might seem unsavory to most but keep in mind, the Madonnas that made the standards for beauty during the classical art period were all wasted when they modeled for those pictures.

"That rum was something wicked," she muttered through heaves.

I slid my credit card into the machine and paid for our meal. The mechanical arm handed me a bag filled with four burgers and a large fry.

I opened the bag and Jessica sat up straight and shut the door then peeked into the bag and grabbed one of the paper wrapped burgers. She unraveled the burger and checked under the bun and furled her brow.

"Bastards, this is yellow mustard not deli mustard!"

"Should we give them back?"

"Hell no...drive."

I put my foot on the gas and we zoomed out of the drive-thru toward the beach. I parked up Rocky's street and left the car behind to stake out on foot so as not to stick out like sore thumbs. Under the cover of this deep wet fog, Jessica and I sat on the curb eating our burgers and keeping our sights fixed on Rocky's studio. Sure enough, her light was on inside though not a sound was stirring.

"I hate pickles with a passion," Jessica said through a mouth full of food as she scooped each pickle slice off her slab of meat.

"If you're offering, I'll take 'em."

I cracked open my remaining burger and she slipped her pickles inside.

"Do you think it's likely we'll see something?"

"No, but what's the rush?" I asked.

"I guess you're right...might as well get to know each other a little better...so, what's your family like?"

"They were a bunch of broke immigrants slowly dying one by one with no one being able to afford to take care of them until they died then no one being able to afford their funerals. It's been awhile since any of them have been alive, so I guess what I look for in a girl now is just someone who reminds me of them."

"Ever been in love?" she asked, trying to hide tears in her eyes.

"No, but I was married once."

"You must've loved her."

"If we loved each other, then love isn't a life-long commitment."

"Ah, so if you don't stay with someone till the day you die, then you don't consider that love? Then what would you call a romance that doesn't cross the finish line?"

"*Confusion.*"

Suddenly, we heard a tapping coming from the distance.

"What was tha..."

I wrapped my hand around Jessica's mouth. I could feel her still masticating in my palm.

"*Shhhh...*"

The tapping came from a set of black shoes that belonged to the Ticking Man. He appeared from out of the fog in a black trench coat and fedora and strode into Rocky Rude's studio. Before he opened the door, he looked around to check if the coast was clear then turned the doorknob with a black leather glove. Once he was inside, the light turned off and I removed my hand from Jessica's mouth and stood up and started walking toward the studio.

"Who was that? Where are you going?"

After a few steps in the studio's direction, I turned around and returned to Jessica and pulled her up off of the curb and took her back to my car. I opened the driver's side door and led her into the seat then closed the door and passed her my keys.

"Drive home."

"What? Why? I want to stay here and help you."

"I won't risk you getting hurt...don't argue with me, just go."

"I'm going to the party..." Jessica said, but I had already split away from the car.

When the car was sufficiently far gone, I let Beretta James out to get some fresh air and wielding her, ran into Rocky Rude's studio.

Gun ready, I slowly crept through the door and onto the tile floor until I felt myself step into a substance. Appearing black in the dark, I kept my gun up while bringing my phone's light down to the liquid. It was a thick red hue. I dipped my finger in and brought it to my nose. It was paint. I looked up and followed the liquid trail until it led me to a pool of red paint beneath Rocky Rude's naked, unconscious body. Face down, the paint seemed to seep out of her.

"No," I lamented under my breath.

The light shot on and I turned around and saw the Ticking Man standing by the switch on the wall.

"You're not going to shoot another dart into my neck, are you?" I asked.

"No."

"Is this your work?" I pointed to the corpse.

"No, but quite honestly, I'm surprised you're not more upset," he said, shaking his head.

"Why?"

"Because she loved you."

The Ticking Man walked over to Rocky's body and turned her onto her back revealing a deep hole in her arm.

"Heroin overdose," the Ticking Man confirmed.

"She couldn't have committed suicide."

"You can deny her love but don't deny her motive, kid."

"Did she leave a note?"

"She texted Royce."

"What did she say?"

"The rest of your paintings are in the garage," the Ticking Man waved me over to the garage and I followed him in.

Inside were all of the painted murder victims but with a new sister to join them: Jessica. My sweet girl, dead among the flower patches, a pale corpse in a sea of orange poppy petals, without blood or emotion. Not a scratch on her, the soul had been reaped out of her with more subtle drama.

"Poison," the Ticking Man suggested.

"I have to call her."

"Where is she now?"

"Some party, she left in my car."

"Follow me, I'll drive."

We ran out the studio together, taking cover in the darkness until we arrived at the Ticking Man's black Dodge on the side of the street. We scrambled inside and he took the wheel and stuck his key in the ignition.

"Where are we going?" he asked.

I texted Jessica: *"Where are you?"*

We waited for her to respond, every second ticking down the

Ticking Man's brow. There was nothing. The Ticking Man's gloved hand hovered over the keys in his ignition, ready to book it off of the beach but then the sound of sirens approached from out the distance and from behind us, four cop cars came streaking by toward Rocky Rude's studio. The police swarmed into the scene, guns drawn, not sure of what they'd find.

"Did you tip them off?" I asked the Ticking Man.

"Maybe Jessica did."

A fifth cop car came barreling down our street but stopped short of the studio and parked right in front of us.

"Damn it, kid. You're gonna get me fired," the ticking man groaned.

"I always thought you should be in another line of work anyway."

The cop car's back door swung open and just by the loafered foot and rainbow striped socks that came sticking out, I knew it was Spinoza. He sashayed out onto the street and over to us, leaning onto the Ticking Man's window.

"Another girl gets the ax and for the first time you two are found at the scene, trying to make a run for it. What makes this dead girl different from all the others? I'm dying to know, detective."

"It was a suicide, see for yourself," the Ticking Man answered Spinoza calmly, staring straight through his windshield.

"We got a hot tip saying otherwise," Spinoza rebutted.

"The evidence is empirical and you know better than to trust your source."

"You don't even know who my source is... get out of the car."

For the first time, I heard the Ticking Man sigh, like a cool blizzard breath from out the cavernous lungs of the last yeti. He stepped out of the car and I did the very same.

"Hands on the roof," Spinoza ordered and we both planted our palms flat on the roof of the car.

Spinoza started patting the Ticking Man down, first feeling a suspicious lump in his coat's pocket.

"Any weapons or blades that I should know about in there?" Spinoza inquired.

"Just a syringe," the Ticking Man answered.

He reached in and pulled out a used syringe with heroin coated walls within the glass and a bloody tip on the metal needle.

"I got a problem," the Ticking Man continued.

Spinoza quickly pulled the Ticking Man's sleeves up and saw his arms were clean and unpunctured.

"Not a hole on you, your guilt's for the lab to decide. Just hope that's not Rocky Rude's blood on the needle."

"Like I said, she committed suicide."

"Assisted suicide is still grounds for a permanent vacation in the cooler and this..." Spinoza dangled the syringe in the Ticking Man's face, taunting him with it, "feels like your hot ticket... turn around and put your hands in the air."

The Ticking Man turned around and Spinoza started patting down his shirt, from chest to gut to sides. He felt something snaking up his waist to his chest and pulled open the shirt, popping off a few buttons, to reveal a black wire recording everything.

"What is this for?"

"Personal use."

Spinoza pulled out the wire and retrieved its attached device, examining it carefully.

"This is for live broadcast...who the hell is listening?"

Messing with him now, the Ticking Man started scanning our surroundings, making Spinoza do the same.

"Someone must be policing the police," the Ticking Man suggested.

Freaking out, Spinoza began to unravel under the crushing threat that he was under surveillance.

"Am I being watched?"

"How does it feel?" I asked him.

His eyes kept darting around to every direction. He spun in circles like a top, imagining invisible demons.

"Now you know just as well as I do, detective...that these practices are unbecoming of a government paid official," the Ticking Man said to Spinoza, "It would be a shame if this got out to the common taxpayer," he threatened.

Spinoza got in the Ticking Man's face, aggression being his last resort before submission, "Who do you work for!? FBI? CIA? NSA? MOSSAD?"

"You know the game, pal. You play it too. They created it, that's who..." the Ticking Man patted Spinoza on the head, ruining that perfect blonde crest.

The Ticking Man then got back into his car, unshaken.

"Later, Vic," I waved at him and opened the car's door but found the Ticking Man's hand in my way.

"This cars for winners, kid, and just to let you know, you failed the test. Get a ride with the other loser," the Ticking Man pointed to Spinoza who was still flustered, trying to find the cameras.

"But what about Jessica?" I asked the Ticking Man.

"She'll turn up somewhere, eventually," he shrugged.

The Ticking Man reached over and slammed his door on me. He turned the key in his ignition, revved the engine and shot like a bullet down the street, leaving Vic and I in his dust.

"Now that he's gone...are we really being watched?"

"I am."

"Damn it...I told Maria I was only going out for groceries."

"She won't find out," I lit a cigarette, deciding to be the cooler cat.

"Oh really? She once dug through our department's dumpster and found some hooker's panties then accused me of being her trick. I don't know how you dealt with it for as long as you did, you must have an iron will."

"I'll let you know the secret...smoking," I blew a hit in his face that made him cough.

"If she knew I was with you right now, my ass would be the only thing smoking."

"I need a ride."

"Then get in."

We entered his cop car together and for a moment, it felt like we were partners.

"Where am I taking you?"

"We need to find a girl."

"Who?"

"Jessica Steinman."

"Cool, one moment."

Spinoza lifted up the center console in the car to reveal a computer screen. He typed Jessica's name into a search bar and multiple results appeared, from her address to her social security number.

"Would you like to go to her house?"

"No, she's at some party."

"Says here she's not in any registered auto-car."

"That's because she's driving mine."

"Oh, why didn't you say so?"

Spinoza typed my name into the search bar and out poured all of my information, including my car's status with an option that read: Track. He clicked the option and a map appeared with the correct GPS location of my vehicle. It turned out that she had parked at a house ten miles north.

"Can you tell me the owner of the house?" I asked.

He tapped the house and a bubble appeared with the lease.

"Dante Cronin."

"Get us there as soon as possible," I jumped out of my seat.

"Computer, drive to Illy Robin's Cadillac at twice chase speed."

The sirens shrieked, flashing red and blue. The car drove at seat gripping, jaw jeering, light speed and led us out of the west side into the suburbs, where music was pulsing so hard out of Dante's house that it rattled the cop car's machinery. We killed the sirens and stopped at the house and saw every beer drinking, pot smoking, miniature American flag waving partier out on the lawn ogling at the unpatriotic buzz kill brigade. I opened the door and swung half of my body out until turning to Spinoza.

"You coming with me?"

"Maria would cut off my balls."

"They already belong to her, you might as well."

I jumped out of the car and addressed the party.

"Nothing to worry about folks, we come in peace."

"Yeah right, you pigs take one step on this soil then consider our response an act of patriotic rebellion and homage to the founding fathers via resistance to tyranny," one American spouted.

Spinoza sighed and pulled every shred of youth in him together to summon the strength to join me outside.

"Did anyone call for a pair of strippers?" Spinoza beamed at the party then dropped his trousers.

It just so happened he was wearing American flag boxers underneath. Spinoza raised his pants over his head and twirled them in celebration, "Let me celebrate my freedoms, you narc-bait sons of bitches."

Our audience laughed and gave us the green light to come inside.

"Happy fourth of July, oinkers," they joked.

We stepped onto the lawn and joined the party.

"Jessica's got black hair, a strong but thin body, about five foot seven," I told him so he could keep an eye out for her.

"Already got all that info...one hundred and sixty-eight pounds," Vic assured me.

We wiggled through the gathering to the front door and entered the party inside. As soon as we arrived in the living room, we found Jessica drinking a beer beside her best comrade, Dorothy Royce. She was happily surprised to see me.

"Oh, my God, Illy...I'm so sorry, my phone is dead...were you looking for me?" she asked as she took another sip of beer.

"No, we were just looking for a party," I played it cool and tried to wink but blinked and she laughed so hard that she spat the beer out of her mouth, onto me, while the booze simultaneously leaked out of her nose.

"I fucking love you," she laughed uncontrollably.

I turned to Dorothy Royce, "Does your father know you're here?"

"He sure does but he doesn't have any clue you were invited... Jessica told me all about your case..." my eyes darted toward Jessica, "Don't be mad, if it wasn't for her I wouldn't have asked the killer you're looking for to throw this party. You won't have to look hard to find something incriminating."

"Surprise," Jessica smiled.

"You think your father had something to do with the killing of all these girls?" I asked Dorothy.

"Obviously," she answered.

For the first time, I felt the gravity of all their deaths. Dorothy put her hand on my shoulder to comfort me.

"It's not your fault, Illy. My Dad's always had skeletons in his closet...you should be happy...we're here together...now...we're young and we're all in love with love."

"Are you on something?" I plunged into her cavernous pupils and soon found myself sinking in.

"Yeah, got some E from Dante. Want me to take you to him?"

"Please."

"Follow me."

Dorothy took my hand and I took Jessica's. Jessica took Spinoza's hand and off all four of us went on our merry way to the bedroom. We opened the door and on the bed was Dante, holding a Japanese katana and smoking a Pacifica beside a German shepherd lying next to him. His feet were propped up so I could see the soles of his size twelve and a half black leather Gizmo boots from which Adolf Hitler was winking at me.

"Who invited the freak?" Dante hissed.

Stumbling onto a killer is never an accident, you hover around their circle and eventually their scent starts pulling you. Spinoza and I both looked at each other, with Eureka spelled across our faces. This was it, every piece of evidence was laid out for us by the Gods and all because Jessica butted into my date and led us here. That's how I knew she was the one.

"A lawman never needs an invitation," Spinoza answered Dante on my behalf.

The German shepherd stood up, crested his back, and started growling at us with grizzly intensity.

"No law breaking going on under my watch, gentleman...you ought to just move along and find a place to make out and watch the fireworks together."

"I'm not his boyfriend, Dante," Spinoza flashed his badge, "I'm Detective Vic Spinoza, LAPD."

The German shepherd began barking incessantly and frothing at the mouth as if trained to react this way upon seeing a badge.

"Did you girls really lead these men right into my bedroom?"

"They just followed the clues, boo," Dorothy said.

"The jig is up, Dante. I'm going to take you down," Jessica continued.

"No, Jessica, this is my case, not to mention I'm the one with the gun."

I pulled Beretta James out and pointed her right at Dante's head.

"You think that just because you got a gun that you get to overstep your jurisdiction? LAPD always gets first dibs," Spinoza furled his brow and drew his dame too and together our twin guns were aimed at the killer.

"Don't even think about taking him in and claiming this case as your own, Spinoza."

"I'm just gonna do my job, that okay with you, your majesty?" Spinoza spat back at me.

"Doesn't anyone believe in due process anymore?" Dante pleaded.

"Monty Freed," I said.

"Monty Freed believes in due process?" Dante asked.

"No, Monty Freed is the man whose life you destroyed by burning his face to a crisp."

Dante laughed, "Wow, that's a blast from the past. I forgot all about that guy. How's he doing?"

"Not too good but once I tell him we burned through your face, then damn it, I'll bet every dollar I own that he'll find a way to crack a smile."

"Don't shoot the messenger, pal. I was only following orders."

"How about these orders? Put your hands behind your back, you're under arrest," Spinoza began.

"See, Vic...that's the problem with you cops, you never know when to just throw the book away and shoot," I said, unloading Beretta James, tearing her vocal chords up with every *scat, scat, scat*. This time, I didn't miss once. I left Dante a bloody corpse on the bed, Pacifica burning a hole through his skin after it rolled out of his limp mouth and onto his chest. The German shepherd surrendered, whimpering over its dead keeper.

A solemn silence swept over the room, and Jessica wrapped her arms around my forearm. Death sent a collective chill down our spines, making his presence known. We stood there a minute, saying a silent prayer until I felt a cuff close around my wrist. Spinoza was only doing his job.

"Sorry Illy...but you can't just kill a suspect on my watch and get away with it."

"You're arresting me? Did you get Maria's permission?"

"She won't mind that I lied to her once I tell her I found York's killer. I'm about to become the most celebrating dick in town."

"You're going to take all the credit?"

"Why not? I'm the only reason you're here...bitch about it anymore and I'll throw another charge of resisting arrest on your ass," he smiled at me with authoritarian delight.

"Whatever, let's go," I rolled my eyes.

Just then a loud burst rang through the night.

"What was that?" Dorothy shrieked.

"Get down. These animals won't let us out alive," Vic dove to the ground and covered his head, while the rest of us just stood and calmly assessed the situation.

I looked down at my phone and saw the clock had struck midnight.

"Fireworks," I said.

Vic realized what was happening and rose off the ground. He pulled me out of the bedroom and back into house which had been totally emptied. We joined everyone outside and discovered these fireworks were like nothing anyone had ever seen in previous years. They would scream up the sky then at the moment you'd expect them to burst, they instead imploded into a "smoke screen" that would play a commercial. The first firework played a video of a beautiful woman smiling when her husband walks into frame and kisses her. A logo for Xyrexa, the penile enhancement supplement appeared. The second commercial shot up into the air and exploded into a video of a happy family facing each other in the back seat of a Rutherford van. Again and again, long into the night, the sky lit up like a giant television for thousands of transfixed eyeballs, wishing they could sit closer to the screen.

"I wish I was born in another time...when life still felt real," Jessica said to me, staring up at the show.

I couldn't bear her implication, that what we had was fake, that we were fake. I knew there was only one way to make us real. I put my cuffed hand on her cheek and turned her away from the sky to me. My eyes, like stars, stared into hers and I kissed her. Now plugged into each other, I sent my rebuttal through the nerve endings in her lips to her brain. I could feel her mind changing and when she pulled away, she kept staring into my eyes and said, "Never mind...this is exactly when I want to be."

Like every Disney princess movie, love would be born in the foreground of fireworks, no matter how hard the powers that be try to pervert everything that makes poor people feel alive. But then squashing the moment like he always did, Spinoza pulled me by the cuff toward the car. Jessica grabbed my other arm and matched Spinoza's strength to pull me back.

"You're not taking him," she shouted.

"Ms. Steinman, if you want to go to jail, I'd be happy to accommodate you."

"Go ahead. It would be a night I'd never forget," she said as she spat into Spinoza's face.

Spinoza blushed so red that the spit nearly turned to steam. He took the second cuff and latched it onto Jessica's wrist, binding her and I together. Any other girl, in any other situation, I would've forced her to let me go to jail alone, but if Jessica was in a cell, I knew she'd be safer than out in the world where Royce or one of his cronies could get to her.

"Awesome," she said as she lunged into me and we vigorously started making out.

"Let me show you love birds to your cage," Spinoza pulled us both to the car to a hail of oinks and empty beer cans from every partier watching on. We were thrust into the cop car's backseat as Spinoza took the front. We zoomed off and for the entire ride, we clung together as tightly as we could. Begging for the police's brutality, only the use of excessive force could pull us apart.

Chapter Fifteen

The Art of Being Tough to Swallow

It took four badges to break us up but once separated, they maced Jessica and escorted her dragging body to a cell. As for me, the cops decided this was the perfect opportunity to let out some steam on a subversive. One cop used his own badge as a weapon and punched me with it over his knuckles, leaving a brand on my cheek. They sent a flurry of swift kicks to my ribs in the hopes I might reconsider my career.

"Private eye, huh? You enjoy taking jobs away from the boys?" one officer barked before connecting.

They beat me to the point they had to carry me into the station. Still conscious, they threw me in the Independence Day drunk-tank. My body and head throbbed relentlessly as the drunks sang this country's original national anthem:

And where is that band who so vauntingly swore,
That the havoc of war and the battle's confusion
A home and a Country should leave us no more?
Their blood has wash'd out their foul footstep's pollution.
No refuge could save the hireling and slave
From the terror of flight or the gloom of the grave,
And the star-spangled banner in triumph doth wave
O'er the land of the free and the home of the brave.

The off-key choir's singing drilled through my ear, rattling my skull. Thankfully, my body was so overwhelmed by the pain and noise that once the throbbing peaked, I just shut down and passed out.

~ * ~

I woke up to a bright, white light bouncing off every square inch of wall, floor, and ceiling to penetrate my eye holes with such intensity that even while shut, it was like staring at the sun. My pupils shrunk to the size of two grains of sand then a door opened up and Detective Holt entered. She was wearing a lab coat and seemed to have lost weight and gotten a nose job since our last meeting.

"Test subject number two, welcome to the Serenity Institute for Rehabilitation or SIR for short."

"Why am I here, Detective Holt?"

"You were brought here by order of your owner and please refer to me as Doctor Holt," she answered and I squinted because the white light was blinding me.

"I can barely see you, please kill the lights."

"I can't do that but don't worry, you'll get used to it."

"Why does everything have to be so white?"

"It's white because the color has yet to be input, would you like it to be another color?"

"Blue."

"Light or dark?"

"Slightly dark, please."

Doctor Holt snapped her fingers and her painted fingernails transformed the same shade of blue as the walls, ceiling and floor. My pupils adjusted and opened up an iota or two.

"Am I allowed to leave?"

"Not before you're reprogrammed."

"Why would I need reprogramming?"

"Because you the failed the test."

"What test?"

"The one you have to start over today, number two."

"Can't you at least tell me what I'm being tested on and how I could improve this time around?"

"No."

The door opened and in came Vic Spinoza in a blue lab coat, holding a glass of blue milk.

"Vic, buddy...I know I've been a real dick but please, help me out of here. We can settle like gentlemen," I tried to talk some sense into them.

"We are settling this. There's no better way to put an end to our conflict than wiping your memory clean," he said as if it should be obvious to me.

"Wiping my memory?"

"Wouldn't be the first time," Detective Holt continued. "Mr. Robin, you're actually an alien being that had his memory wiped then was sent to this prison planet we call Earth as punishment for your heinous crimes."

"What?" I didn't want to believe what she was telling me, but in this situation my disbelief was not only suspended but shattered.

"She's just fucking with you," Spinoza said as Holt laughed. "Here, drink up."

Spinoza brought the milk to my lips, but when my brain instructed my arms to push the glass away, I realized I was completely powerless and unable to move. My mouth opened to let the soothing liquid down my gullet until the glass was empty. He then pulled the glass away.

"I'd like to speak to the Overseeing Voyeur," I said.

"Ovid is at school right now. He will be here after your surgery."

"Surgery?"

"It's just a minor implant replacement procedure, nothing compared to your history under the knife...you were done a great disservice being born into this life in the first place. Those who employ us have found in their gracious hearts the mercy to give you the chance at happiness."

"Disservice being born? Because I'm a cripple?"

Spinoza pulled his hand back, winding it up then snapping it forward to slap me across the face so hard that it loosened my milk coated teeth.

"Achhhh...Jesus...fuck," I seethed with pain.

"I'd never slap a cripple...you're a freak, there's a difference."

"When Randolph Royce sent you on all of those dates, he said you would be rewarded with self-love, do you remember that?" Doctor Holt asked.

"Yes."

"Well do you feel the love?" she continued.

"All I feel is the pain of my fucking face after being slapped into putty," I said while spitting blood.

"If you don't feel the love, then you won't miss it once it's gone."

"Because I won't remember it?"

"The memory wipe is the first step."

"It won't make me forgot about the best thing that ever happened to me. You'll have to kill me."

"Maria is not the best thing that's ever happened to you, Illy," Spinoza said.

"I'm talking about Jessica, you idiot."

"So, you do feel the love?" Doctor Holt realized.

The only love I felt was the all-consuming love that is in sleep, God's merciful coping mechanism for man to escape the horrors of waking life, second only to the love in merciful death. This spell of drowsiness came on most definitely from the milk. In that sleep, my soul rose to the surface like cream.

~ * ~

I felt outside my body. I became the light itself, everywhere. I saw my body lying on a white bed underneath a white sheet in a white room. White coats made a long incision down my forearm and pinned it open to operate. Under the skin was a metal square with teeth biting into the muscle tissue. They pulled the square out and its teeth tore my flesh upon removal. They then replaced it with a new chip that dug in with a deeper bite. The white coats pulled my skin back into place and stitched up over my upgraded hardware. The surgery was a success and the white coats flipped a switch to turn the light off.

~ * ~

When I opened my eyes, I could perceive the changes immediately. I could focus my thoughts on one particular thing and all sorts of information would appear, slightly obstructing my vision with translucent boxes. I stared at my foot and was told the length of each toe nail and when they would need to be trimmed. Options for different pedicurists appeared in order of proximity. I balled up a fist and saw the exact numerical measurement for how much force and heat I was creating.

Doctor Holt entered the room, scribbling on a notepad with a pencil. I focused on her face and gained access to information like her age, income, and cultural background. She did get a nose job.

"Good morning, Mr. Robin."

"Good morning, Doctor Holt."

"How are you feeling?"

"Wonderful, like the happiest new born," my smile shined like I had never smoked a cigarette in my life.

She jotted some notes down on her pad of paper. I could look at the back of her pad and make out each word as it trailed out from her pencil's tip. She wrote, *Delight has increased. Seems authentic for an inorganic. Signs of depression seem to be gone. Libido is at an all-time low.*

"You don't feel upset about Jessica anymore?" she asked.

"Who? I can't imagine I was ever upset."

"I think it's best you not imagine altogether."

"I agree."

"Now, for the first exam," Doctor Holt said as she put away her notepad and pencil.

Doctor Holt slowly took off her lab coat, revealing her pale white arms and freckled shoulders. The lime green straps of her bra stuck out from under her shirt. I stared at the straps and learned the brand and molecular makeup of the bra. Meanwhile, a new bar appeared at the side of my vision measuring my blood pressure. It rose steadily as she proceeded to take off her shirt and bra with one fell swoop, freeing her large bosoms to plop deliciously down to hang loosely, perched atop her stomach. I was given the diameter and weight of each tit. 34DD. I felt a stiffening while multiple alert messages appeared to flash before sight. *Dopamine increased. Serotonin increased. Oxytocin increased. Vasopressin increased. Heart rate 127bpm. ERROR. ERROR. ERROR.*

She took off her blouse and kicked it off her ankle. I lifted the white sheet and looked down at my member. I wish I hadn't because I was better off not knowing the weight, length, stiffness, muscle mass of the hard object. She walked over and propped her leg up onto my bed then hovered her crotch just above my penis. *System crashing. System crashing. Do you wish to abort?* Fuck no.

She pulled her panties to the side revealing her vagina and ever so casually, she took my cock and rubbed it against her clitoris.

"Safe mode or normal?" she asked.

"Normal."

She shoved in the tip, scrambling my mainframe. Prompts appeared in Russian, Arabic, and windings. Different television channels flickered between my penetrating her. *Static, yellow, static, red, static, green. Blurry, blurry, blurry, SHARP.*

She lifted her other leg now and straddled onto me in cowgirl position, bouncing up and down. After a few bounces, my eyes rolled up into the back of my head and I was prompted with an option: Cum or Don't cum. There wasn't even an "or," actually, just "Cum. Don't cum."

"Don't cum," she said, "Wait for me."

I clicked on "Don't cum" but it reappeared immediately.

"Don't cum," she repeated, "I'm almost there."

I followed her instruction and clicked "Don't cum" again but there it was, again.

"Don't..."

"Don't cum, I know," I interrupted her.

I clicked "Don't cum."

"Test subject number two's aggressiveness seems to increase during the act of sex," Doctor Holt stated between short breaths, "Oh my fucking God. I'm about to fucking explode."

She lifted her tit into her mouth and started sucking on her nipple. This sent me over the edge and my screen was flooded with prompts, "To cum or not to cum? That is the question."

Cum.

Cum. Don't Cum. Cum.

Don't Cum. Cum. Don't Cum. Cum. Don't Cum.

Cum. Don't Cum. Cum. Don't Cum. Cum. Don't Cum. Cum.

Don't Cum. Don't Cum. Cum. Don't Cum. Cum. Don't Cum. Cum. Don't Cum.

Cum. Don't Cum. Cum. Don't Cum. Cum. Don't Cum. Cum. Don't Cum. Cum. Don't Cum.

"Now. Do it. Do it. Do it," she screamed as she came.

I clicked cum and my load violently shot up into her. I was given measurements on my seed's viscosity and volume as well as the slight decrease in my own mass. Any measurements of her changes were vague.

She stopped bouncing and just sat there on me. "Test subject number two has cum. Sex lasted approximately three minutes and twenty-two seconds. Internal chemical reading will be imported from the chip. Results will be in shortly. Goodbye, Illy."

Doctor Holt rose off of my body and quickly got dressed, showing no emotion. I could see the milk traveling up the tubes and into my veins. I didn't need it though, she exhausted me.

~ * ~

A wetness between my legs stirred me awake. Still frazzled over what may or may not have happened, I cried and whimpered like a baby, boo-hooing in a ball of my own shame. The cell was unlocked and pulled open by Spinoza, dressed like his regular old self.

"Good, you're awake...here," he passed me a bottle of water which I slapped out of his hand.

"I'm not going back to sleep," I blubbered at him.

He took a closer look, having to squint to really believe what he saw on my crotch.

"Did you wet yourself...? I hope that's piss."

"Leave me alone."

"I'm here to let you go, asshole."

"What do you mean? I killed a man...right in front of you."

"It turns out that you have some friends in high places. That said, I have to apologize... I may have overreacted...and for that I'm sorry. Your actions were in self-defense, after all. Dante didn't have a family or loved ones, anyway."

"Who came for me?"

"Some kid. He should be in school right now but apparently, he's a giant in this city. I don't know how someone his age demands that much respect and power, but my boss tells me he has clearance to say and do anything and go anywhere."

I sat up and wiped away my tears, "Ovid?"

"Yeah, him...he's nothing but a little punk if you ask me."

"Where's Jessica?"

"Ovid told us to let her go too."

I slowly got to my feet, now fully exposing the wet spot on my pants.

"Any chance you keep a spare pair of slacks back there?"

"I can check if there's an extra uniform in storage."

"Please."

Spinoza left me in the cell to stew until he came back with a fresh pair of blue cop trousers that were creased perfectly down the center. Now fresh and dry, I was escorted out of the cell to the lobby where Ovid was waiting for me.

"Where's Jessica?" I asked him.

"I told her to split so the two of us could talk."

"You're not afraid that Royce could get to her out there?"

"I'm indifferent but always watching."

"What did you want to talk to me about?" I asked.

"Can we get a private room and some coffee?" Ovid asked Spinoza.

"Of course, you can but *may you*?" Spinoza corrected the child, "Guess you shouldn't be skipping English class, kid."

"*May we*?" Ovid rolled his eyes before Spinoza led us to a small interrogation room to chat.

I sat down at one end of the table and Ovid took the other.

"Tell me about your dream."

"First, you know about the Disney princesses even though I never told anyone, now you know about the dream too? Get out of my head, Ovid... Get the hell out of my head." I pounded my fists against the table over and over, turning bright red from screaming.

"Calm down, this will all make sense in a moment," Ovid was cool as ice.

I took a few long, hard breaths until I thought I was able to continue.

"Holt and Spinoza performed a surgical procedure to replace a hardware chip in my arm that allowed me to acquire information about everything I could perceive. I could look at your face and know your name, date of birth, interests, anything."

"Was it enjoyable? Effective?"

"It was terrible and frightening."

"The product is still in development, we haven't worked out all the kinks. Can you at least see the potential?"

"The potential threat, yes...is that what this whole test is for? Some new, fangled biomechanical lifestyle device?"

"Hardly. You are the sample in a test for a new genetic modification system in which soul mates are determined upon installation, so that the sample's search for love and happiness has a one hundred percent success rate."

"That doesn't strike you as unnatural?"

"It strikes me as convenient, profitable, and the future. There are too many people in this life who can't find love on their own. Whether they're products of their own insecurities, genes, or victims of society, we have to correct this injustice and bring more love into this world."

"No one's interested in paying for a love like that."

"You'd be surprised, it beats their alternative."

"Whatever, fine...I don't see myself as one who'd want or need a chip just to get a girl, but unless Jessica's not my soul mate, then I didn't fail your test."

"You did fail because she wasn't your soul mate. Rocky Rude was your soul mate, or at least that's how you two were programmed. Your love for Jessica is an error and the result of a statistical impossibility."

"Explain my divorce with Maria, my terrible social skills, my general ugliness?"

"All meant to attract and complement Rocky."

"Were you in cahoots with Royce to get me to that Solstice party where we met?"

"Nope, your shared interests and curiosity led you both to that same place and if it didn't happen there, it would've happened somewhere else, that's how the software works."

"Well, Rocky's dead now so what does that mean for me?"

"It means we have to reboot you...you should be happy about that. We're fixing an error in your code."

"My genetic code?"

"No, your binary code."

Ovid reached into his pocket and pulled out a folded-up sheet of paper that he unfolded and set on the table. The page was filled from top to bottom with zeros and ones.

"Look familiar?"

I studied the page and couldn't find any sort of pattern. It was chaos in its most basic form.

"Why should this look familiar?"

"Because it's you."

He stretched his hand over the table to reach the bottom of the page with his finger and pointed out a sequence:

100100100100001011101010100100100
100100101001010010100101010101010
1010100101010110110101000010101
111111000101001110000001111100

"Right here, this is the error. From subjects one to one hundred, no one exhibits this discrepancy, except you, number two."

"What does it mean?"

"That error is your love of Jessica Steinman."

"I see," I nodded.

"Well I don't...how on earth are you the one exception to our system by subverting destiny as we wrote it and falling in love on your own terms? Your destiny to fall in love with Rocky was literally ingrained in both you."

"So, what you're saying, in a weird way, is I'm evidence love is a product of free will and love is a mystery men shouldn't tamper with."

"No, if anything you're evidence soul mates don't exist...or even souls for that matter. All I'm saying is just when I thought I had the mystery of love solved, you show me I wasn't even close."

"You sound like you ought to hire a detective."

"Maybe...it's too bad we have to start back at the drawing board and erase everything you are to study you as a control."

I coolly lit a cigarette, showing neither resistance nor fear to my authoritarian master and his plans to destroy this reality.

"You can't do that, Ovid."

"Why not? We already own you in every way. You just don't perceive it."

"I'll perceive being without Jessica... I'll know she's out there...and that faint aching absence I'll never be able to pinpoint will influence your data. Face it, I can't be your sample anymore. I don't fit the test's criteria. I'm taken."

"Perhaps you're right.... After all, this whole thing was about making more love in the world. I'm not a monster, I can't do that to Jessica."

"Thank you."

"What I can do though is put you back in the world where you belong and see if you can go all the way with her. Right now, your feelings are nothing but a hunch, big enough to disturb Quasimodo, maybe...but still just a hunch. You were programmed to fall in love this quickly. So was Rocky. Let's see if Jessica reciprocates just as foolishly."

"Where is she?"

"Randolph Royce's mansion."

"WHAT?"

"We let one of his henchmen walk right in and take her to his mansion just to see what you would do right now. This is your final test, Illy."

A stroke of fatherly instinct fell upon me, and I reached my hand back and smacked Ovid so hard upside the head it caused him to fall out of his chair.

I stood up and zipped through the police station, crashing into cops and nearly getting arrested all over again. I reached the lobby then arrived outside where the Ticking Man was waiting for me in his black Dodge.

He whistled at me then shouted, "Need a ride?"

I ran over, opened the door, and quickly hopped in. The Ticking Man then handed me back Beretta James, "Here."

"Floor it," I said, and he obliged.

We zoomed through the city on our way back to the east side where Royce resided in his old Pasadena hilltop mansion. The Ticking Man opened up his glove compartment and inside were two swastikas that he placed onto my lap.

"What are these for?"

"The dogs."

I squeezed the swastikas and they squeaked with adorable menace, "I see."

Running through red lights, wiping through lanes like we owned the street, cutting off the rich and pissing off the poor, the Ticking Man drove like his life was on the line, not just Jessica's.

"What if I can't save her? What if I'm too late? What if I get shot? Even worse, what if Royce is with her, feeling her up?"

"None of those things will happen."

"How do you know? Can Ovid see the future too?"

"No, but we can see Royce, and any amateur gumshoe could take that creep out."

"Will you have my back in there?"

"As an assistant to the test's purveyor, I am not allowed to interfere."

"Driving and arming me isn't interference?"

"Sometimes you have to bend the rules to make sure you stay above water."

"You mean you'll get punished if I muck this up?"

He looked at me and smiled, "I could get killed...but no pressure."

Our car reached the hills and we began winding up the narrow rich man's roads until arriving at the peak where Royce's gates shut us out from the dragon's lair.

"I can go no further. It's all up to you now."

"Wish me luck."

"Good luck and free will."

I nodded and exited out of the car. Immediately, the Ticking Man reversed and peeled out into the opposite direction to fly down the hill. I stepped up to the gates and started climbing, using my cat skills to reach the spiked top. I hoisted one leg over, then two without being caught on one of the points then repelled down to the other side and strolled up the driveway. Hands in pockets and with a solid stride, I knew that Royce was watching me. I could see the front door ahead but then heard two separate barkings coming from either side of the estate. The German shepherds had been released. Rabidly frothing at the mouth, they must not have eaten a thing for days. Just before they came close enough to pounce on me, I reached into my pocket and threw the swastika squeaky toys at them like shurikans. They caught them in their mouths and when they bit down, fast-acting sedative was released and they were put to sleep. I stepped over their fuzzy bodies and made my way inside the mansion.

It felt cold and empty inside until I took a few steps forward and heard a single violin playing an effeminate requiem in the next room over. I followed the lure and came up to a familiar face on a dead body dressed in a tuxedo and propped up to be playing the violin, only the music was coming from a speaker inside the instrument. It was Monty Freed, dead and more comfortable in his skin than I had ever seen him.

"Son of a bitch," I murmured.

I caressed Monty's face and his burn felt cool and in harmony with the rest of his flesh. Suddenly, the music stopped and through the violin's speaker I heard Randolph Royce's voice.

"It was only a matter of time until you found me out, but before you come after me, ask yourself this, is saving Jessica and getting justice for all those girls really worth going down the rabbit hole and exposing yourself to the madness of my mind? I swear you will never be the same after learning the truth that I live with. So, unless you want your mind shattered before dying, I suggest you head back and forget this ever happened."

"If it's not me who takes you down, it'll be Spinoza. I'll be damned before I give him the pleasure."

"Fair enough, have it your way. Come upstairs, we're waiting for you."

I looked over to the red carpeted marbled stairway and made my way up. My hand glided up the balustrade until I saw blood sliding down it and pulled my hand away. I reached the top and suddenly heard more music to guide me. *A dime a dame, but I only have a nickel, what to do in such a pickle? Find a dame that ain't so fickle...*

I followed the song's source to a door that was slightly opened and inside I saw the gallery. Every painting of the dead girls I dated along with others I never knew were hanging on the wall of the circular room and underneath each canvas was a white candle burning in their memory. The last painting was of Jessica and seeing it, again made something in me snap. I raised my gun in the air and just fired. *Scat, scat, scat.* Pieces of ceiling fell to the ground at my feet.

"I won't let this happen again, Royce. I'm taking my life into my own hands, damn it. If you do so much as harm a single hair on her body, I will use your brain as a urinal cake, understand, motherfucker?"

I heard a laughing over the loud speakers that was unmistakably rich.

"That's more like it, the further you go the crazier you get," Royce heckled.

"Show yourself."

"Fear not, I'll be more naked in front of you than I've ever been before."

"I'm losing patience."

"That's not all...sweet Illy, lend me your ears..."

"Fuck you."

"I don't understand where this hatred for me comes from. We're the same, you and I. You came here to get revenge. Well, all these girls hanging in the gallery, their deaths *were* my revenge."

"For what?"

"Rejecting me."

"*Really?*" I couldn't believe his pettiness, or actually I could. All it takes is one rich man's insecurity to ensure the deaths of others.

"That's right...the man that's supposed to have everything. A fifty-story office building downtown, more money than you can ever dream of, a mansion in the hills, a villa in Italy, a chateau in France, a beach house in Jamaica, what more could anyone want?"

"Love?"

"I had that but she divorced me...you know how that feels...you were supposed to sympathize but instead you stole my ex-wife's successor," I could hear him blubbering over the loud speaker. "You don't understand...it's so hard to be rich," he continued.

I had to shut my eyes and take a deep breath out of frustration.

"It's a lie...all of it..." Royce somberly added.

I was too bothered to reply. I just kept quiet.

"Money can't buy love...I lied about all those girls I set you up with. I never slept with any of them. They used me and didn't even enjoy my company, but that's how it goes for all of us rich guys. Love is an invention of the poor, of course it requires hard work to attain and that's something I know nothing about. The rich get so many options that love is reduced to nothing more than a party favor... I would give everything I own to take back the woman that you stole from me."

"She was never yours."

"She will be."

The gallery's second door creaked open, begging me to enter. I walked inside and discovered the room was an indoor meadow, filled with bugs and hummingbirds, flying over the grass and poppy flower covered floor. The unmistakable scent of a woman's sleep filled the air. Among the orange poppies was Jessica, lying naked and still. For a moment, my eyes welled up with tears and my heart sank into my stomach. I ran over to her side.

"Jessica...no..." I softly whimpered.

I caressed my hand against her cheek and felt the warmth of her blushing rush up into my fingers and kill any doubt of her living.

"Jessica?"

Her eyes stirred beneath their lids and her puffy lashes fluttered open.

"Illy, he gave me something that made me sleep," she croaked out in a delirious drawl.

"Do you feel okay?"

"I feel amazing," she smiled, clearly doped up.

"I didn't hurt her," I heard Royce's voice and lifted my head to see him standing naked at the doorway and pointing a gun at me. His penis was shriveled and shrunken and hidden in his orange bush. "I won't, so long as you let me fuck her."

Just then, Jessica sat up and turned to Royce, her fury breaking through her high.

"*You're* asking *him* for permission to fuck *me*? There's no way in hell I'd ever fuck you, Randolph," she settled it that simply.

"You mean you're rejecting me too?"

"Rejecting is too light a word...I'm shutting you down, asshole and don't bother asking out another woman ever again. None of us want you. You're a fucking creep with a small cock."

"What's an old loveless creep to do?"

"Castrate or kill yourself."

"Fine...I'll take the high road."

Randolph Royce's hand shook as he pointed his weapon at me. His unsure, unstable finger tremored on the trigger. I looked him in the eye and caught him in a moment of vulnerability as tears glazed over each ball, giving me the chance to reach for Beretta James. I was too late though. Before I could fire off a shot, Royce took Jessica's advice and raised his gun below his chin and fired up into his skull. The bullet barreled through his jaws and busted into his brain, bouncing around inside his skull like a pinball and spilling red and pink slurry out every exit like a faucet. He dropped like a brown bag of red potatoes.

"Bastard stole my shot."

"If anyone asks, I'll say you did it."

I smiled and we both went in for the kiss, sharing the most beautiful moment Royce's dead eyes could ever witness. We would've gone all the way, but the corpse was staring at us, killing the romance. Randolph Royce was a creep in death as in life.

Chapter Sixteen

Aftermath

Within hours, the news broke that Randolph Royce was dead and responsible for the murders of numerous men and women who crossed him. Within days, my face was all over the news, and I became a bona fide hero, getting offers for interviews and speaking events. The families of all the deceased women pooled together their spare change to give me a proper reward for my troubles. Altogether, they were able to raise two million dollars to change mine and Jessica's lives for as long as we were together, and after four months of dating, I have a good feeling calling that forever. We discussed what to do with the money and decided that I just sit on it and quit the detective business for the only thing that was as subversive, writing. The first action in this transition was to sell my office space. I drove over there to pack my things.

All I took with me was a cardboard box. I filled that box with my old case files, ash tray, office supplies, and the half handle of warm Jameson I kept in the bottom drawer. The last thing I was expecting was a knock at the door.

"We're closed," I said for the first time in my life.

"Illy, it's me," Maria's voice came through the door.

"Oh...come in."

She stepped in, carrying a new presence, now blonde and minus the bangs, the straight and narrow lifestyle changed her. She was a cop's girl.

"Long time no see," I started.

"I figured with all your new popularity, you didn't need me coming back a second time to bother you."

"What bothered me was never getting a thank you."

She walked over and saw the box filled with all my possessions.

"You're not selling the office, are you?"

"Yep...and quitting the business."

Maria sulked around for a bit, unsure of what to say. I could tell she knew she had improved my life with this case and though the thought of my happiness must've bothered her a little, she wouldn't let it get to her head. I knew she was ready to move on too.

"Ugh, Vic is going to be so upset," she shook her head.

"Yeah, right."

"No really, he always tells me how you brought out the best in him."

"Competition will do that."

"If you quit, he gets to have the whole plate of Los Angeles crime all to himself."

"Tell him to wash that plate down with a stiff drink and cheer my retirement."

She stepped in close, vague traces of the past on her breath.

"Do you ever miss what we had?"

I looked at her and smiled, "No...you?"

"No...but I still remember."

"Me too."

"Vic is going to ask me to marry him soon."

"Are you going to say yes?"

She nodded.

"Cool."

"What about you?"

"I don't believe in marriage anymore, just commitment...now if you'll excuse me, I'm done here."

"Thank you, Illy. Take care."

"You too and hopefully the third time's the charm."

I winked, picked up my box of possessions and together we walked out my office and I locked up. We stepped out onto the street and went our separate ways. I set the box down and lit it on fire. Slowly but surely, I watched the flames rise as I opened up the bottle of Jameson. I took a sip for myself then doused the flames with the rest. The flames danced while burning and separating my memories into new substances. Carino caught sight of me from up the street and ran over.

"Hey Illy, what's cookin'?"

"The detective business."

"No way. You're quitting?"

"Sure am."

"You always said without private detectives we'd be living in a police state."

"I still believe that, but I'd rather be a writer. Eventually, someone's going to pick up one of my detective novels and get the same hair brained idea I did. I'm too old and in love for this shit."

"Don't forget you still owe me a favor."

"Shoot."

"I can ask for anything, remember?"

"Lay it on me."

"I want you to leave L.A."

"What?"

"You and Jessica have a future. This place is the past."

"It's all I know."

"Very soon it will become something you don't recognize at all. I'm sure of it. I'm as sure that this city will descend into total chaos as I'm sure I'm breathing right now before you."

"Chaos?"

"The weather and income inequality will only be pushed further to their extremes. The only ones who will stay are the ones too poor to escape, like me and the ones still holding on to the dead dream, like you, if you don't leave. People were never meant to settle in a desert on a fault."

"Where would I go?"

"New York. Where else? You can afford it now."

"I'm not cool with the cold."

"You're not cool with the rich either but you'll change...you already have."

"Love will do that to a guy."

"Go forth, Illy Robin, you owe it to me to never show your face around here again."

I looked down at my burning box and could swear I saw my own reflection in the flames. I looked back up to Carino, who's hand was already out and waiting to be shook. I stuck mine out and paid him back the favor.

"See ya later, buddy. Send me a snow globe," he smiled.

Chapter Seventeen

New York 2025

I took Carino's request to Jessica and she confessed she shared his worries. New York was no little league game though. If we went in with two million dollars to our names, we would have to find high paying jobs quick to survive for longer than a year. Always the gambler, with my life and money, I decided going all in was the only way to go. The good fight had been won on the western front, but from a high rise, looking down on a new city, I could write the great American epitaph and who knows, maybe the call to mystery would be met with new found curiosity. We packed, sold Jessica's grandfather's house, prepaid our one hundred-thousand-dollar entrance toll electronically, and booked a flight to New York. Sitting in the plane that evening, watching it run down the strip then take off, I could see the city I had grown out of for what it really was. Below me was a circuit board grid of tungsten and LED lights with green baseball fields sprinkled between each cluster of gray industry. None of it meant anything. I thought to myself, *The future is now, and the future is sterile and cold and killing us.* I remember imagining I was imaginary but now, holding Jessica's hand in mine, I realized it was the city that was imaginary. As soon as the plane crossed the city limits, the L.A. oasis disappeared behind us like nothing more than a desert mirage.

Our plane landed at JFK airport by sunrise and the city glowed with the radioactive reaction of the smog fucking the fresh morning dew. After picking up our baggage and calling for a car to drive us into the city, we reached the toll booth and were cleared into the pearly gates of Manhattan. Jesus Christ once said that it was easier for a camel to go through the eye of a needle than it was for a rich man to enter the kingdom of heaven. Presented with this problem, it was up to the rich to make their own heaven, out of steel and glass by the sweat of the superior poor. New York is eternity in a bottle.

The sidewalks were filled with the rich. The roads were filled with the rich. The subways were filled with the rich. Jessica and I were rich. The air smelled like freshly printed cash. We arrived at our hotel and I smoked the most expensive cigarette of my life on the fire escape. I scanned the street for any sign of poverty and thought I saw a hand sticking out of a manhole, grabbing at a piece of sandwich left on the ground.

Epilogue

It's been a year since we settled in New York, and Jessica and I are still together and living the good life. I wrote a book and though the publisher was leery about buying it at first, thinking no one wanted to hear stories of rejection and I needed to rewrite it with me sleeping with all my dates, even still, my name recognition carried the novel into enormous success from coast to coast.

Success has its own set of problems, though. Now the police avoid me like the plague, I could be mugged in the middle of Times Square and no one would come to my rescue.

I held a book signing for my latest novel, *The Princess Killing King* and while my head was buried in the books, autographing away, a familiar voice summoned my chin up while pushing his copy under my nose.

"Sign it to the Ticking Man," he winked.

Now with a scar that ran up his face and through his eye, he still intimidated me to the point of a pandering smile.

"Johnny, what are you doing here?"

"I have an offer for you, one that I would rather propose over lunch."

"I have to check my schedule."

"It's clear," he smiled, already knowing.

I signed his book and handed it back to him. He opened it and saw that I had written, "four thirty p.m. at Salvador's Pizza in Little Italy."

We met there, in a booth, with an authentic New York style pepperoni pizza between us. I arrived first of course, and the Ticking Man came moments later, as if he had been waiting to arrive second all day.

"How's Los Angeles?"

"Hot."

"Have you kept in contact with anybody?"

"Nope, I haven't worked for Ovid in months... I have a new profession, that's why I asked to meet you."

"Spit it out, what's your proposal?"

"I'm in the movie biz now and represent some very rich people that would like to turn your story into a film. George Clooney has expressed interest in playing Randolph Royce."

"What about my character?"

"Don't know yet, it's hard to cast someone with your particular set of..."

"Disorders?"

"Physical attributes...is film anything you've thought about before?"

"Not really...to be frank, I can't accept the offer."

"Why not?"

"Movies these days are just too...*high key*... I mean, the way I see it...there's no way you wouldn't fuck this up."

About the Author

Robert Shepyer is a writer that blends the macabre and humorous in a way that will make you laugh so hard that you will squirt black milk out of your nose. With a tone that marries adult nightmares with children's cartoons, he tries to soften the suffering he sees in the world by translating it into a caricature of its worst self.

Bacchus Death Collective

Bacchus Death Collective is the story of a Bacchic death cult of Manhattan elites that are trying to shift the world's current Judeo -Christian value system into a Roman/Hellenistic value system based on the Roman god of wine and hedonism, Bacchus. The nine members of the collective are doomed to a specific death in order to fulfill a prophecy that will usher in the Bacchic age. The prophecy;

"One must die by fire, one must die by frost, one must die by poison, one must die by hanging, one must die by drowning, one must die by eating, one must die by being eaten, one must die by lust, one must die by suicide, one must survive and all must live in praise of Bacchus."

www.ingramcontent.com/pod-product-compliance
Lightning Source LLC
Chambersburg PA
CBHW060434130626
46555CB00005B/2349